12 DAYS OF
FOREVER

12 DAYS of FOREVER

HEIDI MCLAUGHLIN

Cover by: Sarah Hansen / Okay Creations
Models: Candon Rusin / Madison Rae
Editing: Snow Editing
Formatting: Tianne Samson with E.M. Tippetts Book Designs

BOOKS BY
HEIDI MCLAUGHLIN

The Beaumont Series

Forever My Girl Beaumont Series #1
My Everything Beaumont Series #1.5
My Unexpected Forever Beaumont Series #2
Finding My Forever Beaumont Series #3
Finding My Way Beaumont Series #4
12 Days of Forever Beaumont Series #4.5

Lost in You Series

Lost in You Lost in You #1
Lost in Us Lost in You #2

The Archer Brothers

Here With Me

CHAPTER 1
YVIE

"WOULD you care for a warm towel, ma'am?"

I blink and turn my focus to the flight attendant pushing her wet towel in my direction. I take it and smile at her as my thanks. I don't know what to do with it, but others are wiping their hands. I opt to cover my face and let the warmth seep through. I was hoping that my mind would focus on the hot cloth lying on my face, but it doesn't.

I'm escaping. At least that's what Oliver tells me. We've been together off and on now for over a year, and lately it's been more off than on. He says it's me, but dating the producer of my Broadway show, *Enchantment*, has never been my cup of tea. I want to earn my way. I want the lead based on my ability as a dancer, not because of who my boyfriend is. He doesn't understand that. He says that he loves me, but right now I'm clearly in the "like" stages of life. I'm not sure he's the one, but I'm drawn to him and I don't know why. I thought that it was because he was older, and I felt he was more sophisticated, but lately that hasn't been enough for me to give him my heart. Something's missing, or I'm just not into him and I need to admit it and move on.

The fear is there, though, that he'll cut me from the show because I'm no longer with him and replace me with a younger dancer. I think about it all the time and wonder if I'll land another gig. He's said the words that cut deep: my ass is too big, my toes don't point, and my bun isn't high enough. He follows up with an "I love you" but the sharp edges of his words still hurt. I work harder following those fights. I spend more time in the gym, longer hours in front of my barre working on my form. The bun I can't help until my hair grows longer, but I try and that's all I can do right now.

The captain's voice comes over the intercom. It's jumbled, but we all know what he's saying. We're about to land. In under an hour I'm going to see my nieces and nephew. I'll get to wake up to their joyful laughs on Christmas morning and tease my brother relentlessly when he tries to sneak a kiss with Katelyn.

Harrison doesn't know I'm coming. I'd like to say it's a surprise, but the truth is I just needed to get away. Spending time with him, Katelyn and the kids appealed to me more than staying in his beachside apartment alone. My mom will be in Beaumont for Christmas too, and I miss her. I really just need my family right now.

I remove the now cold, wet washcloth and return my chair to its upright position. The moment we were allowed to recline, I did. With no one behind me, the freedom to relax and reflect was much needed. Once the plane touches down and is at the gate, everyone is out of their seats and scrambling to get their carry-ons from the overhead lockers. It's almost a race to stand-up. The only winner is the person in the first class seat. They're calling all the shots because plane etiquette dictates that those of us in the cheap seats have to wait our turns. Some people don't abide by the rules, and when I see them I just want to stick out my foot and trip them. Mean, I know, but whatever.

With my bag gathered, I shy away from looking at the families excited to see their loved ones. Harrison would've been here if I had told him I was coming, but I didn't want to interrupt his family time. He's changed so much since he met Katelyn, and it's all been for the better. She's the sister I never thought I'd have, and she's given me two exceptional nieces.

I think I'm homesick. My mom is always talking about Quinn, Peyton and Elle and how much fun she's having, how her life feels almost complete. I know she's spending more and more time in Beaumont now that Harrison has a family. I'm not jealous. I'm not anywhere near ready to have a family, but I do miss Quinn and I want to really know the twins. I enjoy my role as an auntie, but I am missing too much. Email, text messages and the odd Skype call just aren't cutting it for me anymore.

Moving isn't an option. Beaumont doesn't have anything to offer me unless I want to quit dancing. I could open a dance studio and teach ballet, but that isn't my dream. I can feel my dream within my grasp so giving up now would likely just depress me. Maybe I could convince Harrison to spend a few months in New York. The kids could get a tutor, Katelyn and I could shop and Harrison could work with Oliver's production company. It'd be a win-win for me, but probably not for them.

It's incredibly selfish of me to think they'd uproot their lives and come to New York because I'm homesick.

It's easier for me to do it, to move to Beaumont and be a part of a larger family. I could get to know Noah and Josie better, babysit Eden and maybe teach her ballet once she turns three. What Harrison has here is real. They're all a close-knit family, and I'm just observing them from afar.

This is exactly why I needed a break. My head is swimming, and I know that once I see everyone, after I give it a few days, my mind will be back to where it needs to be: focused on my goal. I'll be levelheaded and fully functional when I return to New York after New Year's. Oliver won't know what hit him when I take the stage. I'll be in shape, just the way he expects me to be. I'll be en pointe and deliver every step of the routine without faltering.

I pull my hire car into the driveway and park. The lights are on in the house, and there are shadows moving behind the curtains. Harrison is probably wondering who just pulled into his driveway so late. He's going to be worried, scared even, that something is wrong. I've never shown up unannounced before. This is out of the norm.

Harrison and Katelyn's house is huge. Her former father-in-law gave it to her so her girls could live in the house in which their father was raised. My brother is the most generous man I know. From the pictures I've seen, there are family photos of Katelyn's former husband everywhere, and he's talked about all the time. Ever decision they make, they do so with Mason's beliefs in mind. My brother has made it his mission to keep Mason's spirit alive for the twins. And I think for Katelyn and Liam, too. I'm not sure there are too many men out there that would do that. When I think about it, Oliver would be completely against how Harrison lives. Maybe that's a sign he's not for me.

Before I can put one foot on the step, the front door

opens and the tall, looming figure of my brother emerges.

"Yvie? What are you doing here?"

I shrug and take the steps until I'm level with him. "I needed a break, I guess."

Harrison gives me a half smile. "So you thought you'd come to a house with three loud kids?"

I can't help the tears that start to glisten my eyes.

"Hey, what's wrong?" he questions softly.

"I think I'm homesick. I don't know. Oliver and I haven't been getting along and the show is on hiatus until after the New Year. I packed a bag this morning and caught the first available flight out. All I could think about was waking up on Christmas morning with Quinn. The last couple of years have been really hard when he wasn't home, and I couldn't bear another year without him."

Harrison pulls me into his arms, holding me to his chest as tears fall from my eyes. I'm such a girl, crying because I missed everyone. I know most of my emotions are coming from my failed relationship, but seeing Harrison has really brought it all out of me.

"Hey Dad, Mom says we're not heating the outdoors."

I pull away at the sound of Quinn's voice. His eyes go wide and brighten when he sees me. "Auntie Yvie!" he shouts with such joy that my response is stuck in my throat. He's happy to see me.

Quinn wraps his arms around me just as I bend down. This hug is what I needed. I needed to feel the love that this little boy has for me and to be able to give it back. Maybe this is what I've been missing these past few months.

My family.

CHAPTER 2
XANDER

BUNDLE the collar of my coat tighter around my neck as I walk against the wind. For the most part the weather is Beaumont is mild, but we do get these days when it's so cold the wind chills your bones. It only lasts for a few days and right now we're going on day three of one too many. This is my first winter in Beaumont. I didn't have a lot of expectations when I moved here, but I was hoping for a calmer winter. I can't complain though. I have A-list clientele and a thriving business. Being the only gym in town can do that for you, especially when I'm keeping my rates low and my hours flexible. I'm catering to the working class, both men and women.

Beaumont is a mix of blue- and white-collared workers, and I'm working to meet their needs. I've been able to hire a full complement of staff, and that enables me to dedicate myself to personal training and physical therapy. Most of this is in part to landing a lucrative deal with local band 4225 West. They're based out of Beaumont, but I'll be travelling with them when they go on tour in the spring. It's mostly due to precaution with their keyboardist, Jimmy Davis. He was shot and almost died when a bullet ripped through his lung. He was in a coma for about a month and had extensive physical therapy to regain his full lung function.

Opening the door to *Whimsicality*, the scent of Christmas hits me hard. I'll be staying home during the holidays so I can give my employees the time off. They have families, and all I really have are the Westburys, James' and Davis'. I've been invited to spend Christmas Eve and Christmas Day with them, and I've accepted. I enjoy hanging out with them, but it does make me long for something more. My parents married young, and I always thought I'd follow in their footsteps. But life has a funny way of steering you down the path you least expected. I can't complain though because I'm happy. I own a successful business, some of it thanks to Liam, but mostly because I know what I'm doing.

Whimsicality isn't crowded, mainly because of the expansion it recently went through. When the business next door ceased trading, Liam and Josie purchased that space, making the café larger. The band plays here occasionally, which brings in a lot of fans. They play impromptu shows and use social media to tell fans when they're happening. Right now, *Whimsicality* is decorated for the holidays. There's a Christmas tree in one of the corners and lights everywhere. Garland hangs on the walls – I know it's garland because I was asked to help to hang it. We spent a Sunday in here doing everything by Josie's instructions while she made those fancy center things that sit on the tables.

I choose to sit by the fireplace to take away the chill.

During the remodeling phase, Harrison uncovered a massive brick fireplace that had been covered in plaster. He worked for hours to clean each brick and even replaced the cement to make it look brand new. It definitely adds to the winter ambience of the café.

"Hello, Xander. What can I get for you tonight?" Dana asks while she sets a cup of coffee in front of me. I'm a regular. I know the menu by heart. Dana has been here for about six months. Once the expansion was done, Liam convinced Josie to hire some help. He wants her to travel with the band when they go on tour this coming spring. She's had a hard time letting go and just being the boss. Katelyn still helps out but not as much. It's mostly while the kids are in school. Jenna stays primarily in the florist shop. Josie finally gave in and hired Dana as well as Sarah and David. David works mostly behind the counter and Dana and Sarah wait on tables. Josie hasn't said anything during our sessions that would lead me to think she's unhappy with the lesser workload.

Aside from the gym, that's the one thing that has been a constant for me – personal training. It started with Jimmy, but Liam liked the idea of the band staying in shape. He also liked the fact that he trusted me enough to help Josie tone up, not that she needed it. I work with the girls three days a week, and the guys four days. That alone keeps my gym in business.

"I'll have the turkey on rye, please."

Dana nods and walks away. She's a cutie and a gym member. She goes to college and works here to help pay for her tuition. Her parents came to the United States when she was three and left her on the orphanage steps before returning to China. She was adopted quickly and has lived a pretty privileged life from what she tells me. She also doesn't resent her biological parents and hopes to meet them someday. I'm not sure how I'd feel if my parents did that, but I understand why hers did – to give her a better life.

The door chimes, and I look over my shoulder to see if I know who's coming in. That's small town life for ya. Everyone knows everyone, or they know your parents, brother or sister, etc. Liam is the shyest person I know, but he knows everyone. We can't walk down the street without someone coming up to him. They either want to talk to him about coaching the high school team, which he's politely declined many times, or they want to ask him when his next single will be out. Rarely does he get asked for autographs; that's all Jimmy. Regardless of the fact that he's married and a dad, he still has girls chasing him, especially on Twitter. He tried to get me hooked on his favorite social media site, but I told him it's not for me. I have my business page and that's about it. My business is simple – I help you get in shape and stay in shape.

Dana brings my food along with a glass of water. She knows that's what I like to drink while eating. I'm here nearly every day. It's better than being home alone and eating in front of the television. If I could, I'd have clients until it was time to go to bed, but no one wants to work out at nine at night.

I'm getting to that point in my life where I want to settle down. I want to find someone to spend my nights with, someone that I can hurry home to at the end of a long day in the gym. I want to walk into my house and feel warmth and comfort. Right now, it's barren and there's no life. I'm a bachelor and actually had to stop myself from putting up my psychedelic posters and plugging in my black light. I don't want to live the dorm life anymore.

I've recently realized that I can't trust a lot of people. The few women I have dated since I moved to town just wanted to get close to the band. I felt bad, but the guys understood. They said it wasn't the first time something like that had happened. So now I'm leery. I have to find someone who wants me for me, not for my client list and at whose house I happen to hang out on the weekends. I need to be enough. Whoever I end up with needs to like kids, too. All my friends have them and those kids are the centers of their universes.

I want that in my life.

CHAPTER 3
YVIE

THE thunder of elephants stomping down the hall is what wakes me. The creak of my door opening and little voices whispering is what gets me to open my eyes and prepare for the launch of Quinn. This time though he has two counterparts that I'm fully expecting to join in with the torture I'm about to receive. I cross my arms over my chest and close my eyes tightly. The bed moves just a smidge, and it's Quinn's voice that tells the girls what to do.

"Like this," he says before he launches himself onto my bed, falling over the top of me. I play dead. It's part of the game.

"Quinn, you killed her!" I don't know which girl is speaking, but she's spot on.

"She's not dead, Elle, she's pretending. Watch," he says as he sets his hands on my hips and starts tickling. I can only fight my laughter for a moment before I pull him into my arms and tickle him back.

"You're supposed to let me sleep in, you little monster."

"But it's breakfast time."

I look over my shoulder to see the twins standing like statues. Elle is dressed in a pink nightgown with her hair in pigtails and holding a doll. Peyton is dressed in shorts and a football t-shirt. Her hair is down, but badly needs to be brushed to smooth the tangles. From what Harrison has told me about them, Elle is more outgoing while Peyton is reserved.

"Do you want to come up here?" I ask them. I want to have the same relationship with them that I do with Quinn. I know that Katelyn is an only child, and I believe Mason was one as well so that doesn't leave them a lot of family options. My brother has adopted them, so as far as I'm concerned they're my nieces.

"Yes," Elle says as she climbs up, but Peyton just stands there. She's watching Elle like a hawk, but quickly turns her gaze to Quinn.

"You can come up, Peyton. Auntie Yvie is really cool."

I sit up, thinking that maybe she's afraid to hurt me. Peyton starts biting her lower lip and her fingers pull on the hem of her shirt. Quinn pats the spot next to him, but she starts taking steps backwards. She's out the door before I can say anything.

"She's shy," Quinn says, shaking his head.

"Is she always like that?" I wonder if I'm going to have to tiptoe around her.

"No, only since Daddy Mason went to heaven. He was her bestest friend, but now she has Uncle Liam and Daddy. They take care of her."

My eyes become a bit misty as I listen to Elle refer to Harrison as her dad. The day Quinn came to us, he became a changed man. He had something to live for, something to prove.

"Mom's cooked breakfast for you. She says you need to come downstairs." Quinn sighs as if breakfast is ruining his day.

"Are you not hungry?" I slide out of bed and wait for them to get off so I can make it.

"I've eaten mine, and I want to spend time with you."

"Me too," Elle says, bouncing on her knees.

"We have plenty of time since I'll be here for week or so. I'm in no rush to go back to New York."

"Are you a really real ballerina?" Elle asks.

"I am, wanna see?" she nods as I get off the bed and rise up on my toes and perform a small routine. She stands on the bed and starts to follow what I'm doing. I watch her from the corner of my eye and think that I could teach dance lessons to someone like her. But that would mean giving up on my dream.

"I want to be a ballerina just like you," Elle yells as she twirls on my bed. I laugh and Quinn rolls his eyes.

"Next week she'll want to be something else."

"Will not," Elle says as she stands on the bed with her hands on her hips. Quinn nods, but doesn't say anything else. "You're a poopy head, and I'm telling."

Elle jumps down and doesn't miss a beat as she storms out the door and starts yelling for Katelyn. Quinn stands there, looking down at the floor.

"What's wrong?" I ask, pulling him into my arms and sitting down on the edge of the bed.

His lips go into a thin line as he rests against me. "Having little sisters sucks."

I laugh, remembering all the times I would torment Harrison. "I'm sure they're not so bad. When I was your age I used to make your dad's life so miserable. He would whine to Grandma every day about how I was in all of his stuff, but he was also my best friend and I knew I could count on him for anything. He protected me." Even when he was unable protect himself from the bullies. I don't add the last part. That's for Harrison to share with Quinn when the time is right.

"Come on, let's go eat some food and figure out what we're going to do today."

"We have school today," he says solemnly.

I scrunch my face in detest. "Fine, after school you're all mine!"

Quinn and I walk downstairs hand in hand and into the kitchen. Their house is huge, especially compared to the house in which we grew up. Even Harrison's apartment in California could fit in here. I suppose, though, with a family of five you need a lot of room.

As we step into the kitchen I pause. Harrison is standing in the middle of the room drinking coffee with Peyton hanging off his back. Katelyn is plating up food, and Elle is sitting at the island playing with her doll.

"Morning," he says, tipping his mug toward me.

Katelyn turns and smiles. "Sorry they woke you up this morning. I told them not to, but Quinn said it was tradition."

I look at him and squint. "It's fine. I should probably be up anyway." I chance a look at Peyton who hides her face in Harrison's neck. Quinn wasn't kidding when he said she was shy.

"Doesn't your back hurt, holding her like that?"

He cocks his head and winks, but Peyton isn't looking at him. "I don't mind. She's pretty light, and I've been lifting weights."

"Excuse me, what?" I ask just as Katelyn hands me a cup of coffee.

"What?" Harrison asks as if him lifting weights is an

every day occurrence.

"You — in a gym — is something I'd have to see to believe."

Katelyn laughs and pulls Peyton off his back. She whispers something to her, and Peyton runs by without saying anything. "Elle and Quinn, go get ready for school, please." The kids disappear upstairs and just like that the kitchen is quiet. I walk over to the island and sit down.

"You okay?" Katelyn asks, and I nod.

"Just… I don't know. I needed a break. The show went on hiatus because *The Nutcracker* will be showing at our theater, and I just couldn't stay there. I missed Quinn, and I want to get to know the twins."

"They'd like that," Harrison tells me.

I shake my head. "Elle, maybe, but not Peyton."

"Give her time. She's leery of people because she thinks they're all going to leave her. She's pretty amazing once she opens up."

I nod and take a sip of my coffee. I add some of the eggs, bacon and toast to one of the empty plates and start to eat.

"What else is going on?" Harrison asks. I swallow and look at my brother. He's leaning on the counter with Katelyn glued to his side. She's looking at him with a pensive expression. I get the feeling that they discussed me last night. Honestly, I expected it. I know I would if someone showed up to my house late at night and then ran straight to bed without explanation.

"I broke up with Oliver, and I'm not sure if I'm on the right path."

Harrison starts to smile until Katelyn elbows him. I roll my eyes. I know he, Liam and Jimmy don't like Oliver – Jimmy made that very clear when they were on tour last time.

"What?" he asks Katelyn.

"Be nice."

"Why? I don't like the guy. I'm not going to pretend that the news doesn't excite me."

I roll my eyes. "Anyway, we're over, and I don't think I'll take him back."

"What'd he do?" Katelyn asks, and I shrug.

"It's me. I'm just not into him."

Before they can grill me for more information, the kids come down all ready for school. There's a honk outside, and they start rushing around. They hug Harrison before dragging Katelyn to the door.

Harrison steps toward me and leans forward. "What's going on?"

I shrug and fight the tears from forming. "I'm not sure dancing is my dream anymore."

My brother smiles and says, "The funny thing about dreams is that they change. You just close your eyes and a new one can play out like an old movie reel with you as its star."

"What are you guys talking about?"

Harrison straightens and Katelyn walks right to his side. His face lights up like it's the first time he's seeing her. I want that. I want to see the love someone has for me shining in their eyes.

"Brother and sister stuff," he says, not needing to respect my privacy, but I'm thankful that he's changing the subject.

"Well, I'm going to call rank and take Yvie to them gym. I have a training session with Xander."

"Who's Xander?" I ask, as I stand and carry my dishes over to the sink.

"Only the hottest single guy in town."

"Hey," Harrison says as he looks at both of us. "I'm

hot and single."

Katelyn and I both start to laugh, and he quickly joins in.

"I know, it was just something funny to say." Harrison says as he kisses Katelyn before taking the few steps to me. He pulls me into his arms and holds me. "You can stay here as long as it takes for you to see your movie play out." He kisses me of the top of my head and walks out of the room.

"I think you'll like Xander. He's extremely hot."

I smile. "Aren't you madly in love with my brother?"

Katelyn shrugs, but never stops smiling. "Doesn't mean I don't appreciate a fine looking man and neither will you."

CHAPTER 4
XANDER

THE gym is bustling with patrons when I walk in at eight. The music is loud, but not uncomfortably so. We open at five-thirty to give those who travel out of Beaumont a chance to get in a workout before leaving for work. The clank of the weights coupled with the whir of the treadmills being run on is music to my ears. I look around and feel a bit nostalgic. I hate thinking that if it weren't for JD getting shot, Liam would've never have put the word out that he was looking for someone to help JD get back on track. I'm just the lucky bastard that happened to be in the right place at the right time and in the right frame of mind when I found out about the opportunity. I needed a change in my life and Liam, unbeknownst to him, opened up a whole realm of possibilities for me.

I shake the mouse to bring the computer alive. My schedule is flexible today, allowing me time to hit the floor for a workout in the hope of gaining more clients. Most people are interested in personal training, but too gun-shy to actually ask about it. They think it's too expensive, and it can be, but I strive to keep my fees comparable to the bigger city gyms. I'd rather keep my locals happy and in my gym then to lose them to the conglomerate chains that keep popping up. Sure they have newer equipment, but I offer individualized training and three of my staff members are working on getting their degrees in personal training.

My first client of the day is Katelyn, and the computer is showing a plus one next to her name. I rack my brain trying to remember if she said she was bringing in someone, but I can't recall anything.

"Hey, Becky, can you tell me why Katelyn James has a plus one next to her name?" Becky was my first hire and manages the gym for me. She's in charge of setting up appointments, memberships, most of the hiring and firing and is my all-around right-hand person.

"I'm not sure. She called this morning and said she's bringing someone with her and asked if that was a problem. I didn't think it would be."

"No, no, it's okay just curious." Before I can put anymore thought into who'd be with her, the door opens and in she walks, followed by Harrison's sister. I know it's her because she's a smaller version of him, just much prettier, although the photos I've seen of her didn't do her any justice. I can't take my eyes off of her, and I follow her every step until she's disappeared behind the door to the locker-room. The fact that I'm staring like a crazed stalker bothers me. I've seen beautiful women before, and even without knowing her, I'm certain she'll end up being like family.

As soon as the girls come out of the locker room changed and ready to go, they pull down yoga mats and start their warm-up. Each of my clients has instructions for their one-hour sessions. They stretch and warm-up for fifteen minutes, I work them out for thirty, and they end with a fifteen minute cool down.

I try to busy myself with any menial task I can find while I wait for them to finish, but I find myself watching Harrison's sister. She's more flexible than any of my clients. Her body is toned and the workout outfit she's wearing is definitely going to catch some attention from the men in the gym. This woman is in shape and takes care of her body. I have a feeling that a few of the women that come in will be jealous. Hell, I am. I'd love to have one of my clients achieve what I'm seeing now.

I push off the counter and make my way over to them. Katelyn smiles as soon as she sees me, and Harrison's sister straightens. She's about average height, not as tall as Harrison. But the word toned doesn't do her justice. This woman is muscular and defined. This woman is a serious athlete, and I'm racking my brain trying to remember if Harrison ever said what she does for a living.

"Xander, this is Yvie, Harrison's sister. Yvie, this is Xander. He's owns the gym and is Jimmy's trainer."

"Well, I train all of you, don't I?" I wink at Katelyn and offer my hand to Yvie. When our hands meet, I hope for that spark, that electricity that everyone talks about when they meet someone they're attracted to, but it's not there. And I want it to be. I've seen a lot of women in my life, but none more beautiful than her. I don't know if it's the way her dark hair contrasts with her emerald eyes or the fact that I can picture her standing next to me at parties and in my kitchen as we make dinner together. I haven't felt the need to get to know a woman just by standing next to her. Her small hand is dwarfed by my much larger one, and I'm shocked to feel just how dainty she is. "It's nice to meet you," I say, as I pull my hand away from hers. I feel as if we lingered in our handshake maybe a little longer than necessary. None of it should mean anything, except that I feel like it does. Do I need a shock or that electrical current? Can't I just *know*? "So, Yvie, what would you like to work on?"

She immediately looks down without making eye contact, which tells me that she has low self-esteem, and for the life of me I can't understand why. Yvie mumbles her answer without looking at me.

"I'm sorry, the music is too loud; could you please say it again?"

Yvie looks at Katelyn and sighs. Her eyes barely reach mine when she speaks. "My ass is too big."

I do what any self-respecting personal trainer would do: I lean to the side and take a good hard look at her much-too-big ass that doesn't freaking exist.

"Excuse me, and I don't mean to be rude, but your ass is fine." I want to smile, but I also don't want to come off as creepy.

Her head shakes slowly. "My producer says it's too big."

"Katelyn, go ahead and get started on your ab routine. I want to talk to Yvie for a few more minutes." I never leave my clients to start their routines without me, but I'm a little confused over Yvie's confession and need to know where she's at if I'm going to offer assistance. Hell, I may be jumping the gun here, but Katelyn brought her in as a plus one so that leads me to believe she wants help. I just don't know how or where I can help her. I signal for Yvie to follow me so Katelyn can get started.

"What do you do for work?" I ask, as I lean against the window. Yvie stands off to the side with her arms crossed over her chest. She doesn't carry that defiant look, as if she's in trouble. She's comes off as if she's protecting herself from something or someone. I study her more, taking in her high cheekbones and her plump lips. I never looked at her photos in true depth before and now I'm kicking myself.

"I'm a dancer, ballet mostly." My guess was athlete, but I noticed something different by the way she walked. I thought it was just me looking for something to sway me from finding her beautiful, but no. She has a reason to walk the way she does, to prance. It's engrained into her system to always be poised.

"That explains your flexibility, but why are you concerned with your...." minutes ago I had no issue saying "ass" but in this moment I'm at a loss for the most appropriate word. I don't want to come off as crass, but then again she does hang out with rockers from time to time.

"Ass, you can say it. You already did over there."

She's sassy. I like her more and more already.

"All right, tell me why you aren't happy with your ass?"

"Like I said, my producer says it's too big."

"He's a moron," I say before I can catch myself. "I'm sorry that was wrong." I run my hand over my hair in slight frustration. Why men insist on being like this toward women I'll never understand.

"It's fine. I agree, but it's my job to look my best, and with Christmas in a few days I know I'll eat my fair share of junk so I don't want too much of a challenge when I get home."

"And where's home?"

"New York City."

And that's why I didn't feel a spark. I already knew she was off limits with her being Harrison's sister, and now I know she's out of my league.

"Well, let's get started on those glutes of yours."

CHAPTER 5
YVIE

KATELYN and I spend the remainder of the day shopping for Christmas presents while the kids are in school and Harrison is in the studio accomplishing nothing. He spent the majority of the day asking where we were and when we were coming home. He kept telling Katelyn that his baby sister was in town and that she was monopolizing my time. Spending time with Katelyn doesn't bother me though. I want to get to know her and feel a bond with her and her girls. They're important to Harrison, and I take my role as a sister and auntie very seriously.

When we finally pull in, she tells me we have to leave the packages in the trunk until after the kids go to bed. Katelyn says that the twins are the worst, always sneaking around and trying to look in the closet for gifts. Hearing her say that reminds me of what I was like when I was little. I hated surprises and absolutely hated waiting for

Christmas morning. I looked for my presents in every nook and cranny I could find, always disappointed that I couldn't find anything. It wasn't until I was much older that I figured out my mom wasn't buying presents until Christmas Eve when most things were on sale because she that's when she could afford it. Harrison never looked. I think it was because he knew but never wanted to say anything to ruin my fun.

As soon as we walk into the kitchen, the first thing I notice is how loud the house is. Their house is somewhat old so the walls are thinner and the noise travels. The television is on in the other room, there's laughter and someone is screaming. Growing up our house was never like this. When Harrison and I came home from school, everything was quiet. We didn't turn on the TV or rummage through the refrigerator. We sat at the table and did our homework until it got dark. Only then would Harrison turn on a light and start making dinner. It wasn't until Harrison had a paying gig and after we moved that I figured out how poor we were. I never knew my dad, but Harrison did an amazing job filling in for him. He took on so much adult responsibility to make sure I had a good life growing up.

Quinn, followed by Elle, comes running into the kitchen. They each attach to my legs, their laughter filling the room. It doesn't faze Katelyn, and maybe that's the 'mom' part of her life. Our house was so quiet that it was almost like we couldn't make any noise. Harrison and I never yelled and we didn't have many toys, so maybe that's the difference.

Harrison walks in, followed by Peyton. She looks at me, but quickly averts her eyes. I'm not sure what I have to do, but I want to know her and wish she were as easy going as Elle.

"Get off your aunt," Harrison snaps and the kids remove themselves immediately. Quinn has always done what Harrison asks right off, but for Elle to do it as well shocks me. I know it shouldn't — he's her dad for all intents and purposes — but the way she lets go without any argument amazes me for some reason.

"They were fine," I say, hoping to diffuse the situation.

Harrison laughs, catching me off guard and I look at him questioningly. "They don't need to treat you like a jungle gym." I glance a look at Quinn and can tell all he wants to do is spend time with me.

"Why don't you and Katelyn go out to dinner and a movie? I can watch the kids."

Katelyn stops what she's doing and looks at Harrison. Her eyes are so wide you can tell they haven't been going out much. Elle and Quinn start jumping up and down, but Peyton doesn't change her expression. Maybe if she and I can spend some time together, she'll relax a bit and trust that I'm not going anywhere. I wish I could tell her that I understand what it's like to lose your dad, but I don't remember. I think that's why she and Harrison have such a bond. They've both been there. They both remember what it's like to have someone ripped away from you.

"Going out would be nice," Katelyn says, and I have to cover my mouth to hide my smile. She's making puppy dog eyes at Harrison while he just stands there. I have no idea what my brother is thinking, but if I were he, I'd be jumping at the chance.

"Seriously, guys, go out and let me hang with my nephew and get to know my nieces. I think I spotted a couple of movies that I wouldn't mind watching, and we can make homemade pizzas."

Both Quinn and Elle start jumping up and down again begging their parents to let me babysit. Harrison looks at me, and I nod until he breaks out his patented smile.

I start clapping my hands and pull Quinn and Elle into me, only to watch Peyton disappear around the corner.

"I can drop her off at Liam's," Katelyn tells me, as if she's reading my mind.

I shake my head. "We'll be fine. Besides, I really want to know her and spending time together is the best way."

"If she's an issue, you'll give us a call?" Harrison asks, and I agree. I won't call them though. They need this time out so they can be a couple.

It doesn't take Katelyn long to get ready, and when she comes downstairs Peyton follows but stops mid-way down and sits on the step. She's holding onto her football, and I remember Harrison saying it was a gift from her dad; she carries it everywhere, especially when she's upset or nervous.

"You guys have fun," I say, as I usher them out the front door. "We'll be fine, and if there are any problems, I'll call." The last part is a lie, but they don't need to know that. I shut the door behind them and lock it, mostly to keep Harrison and Katelyn from rushing back and second-guessing their night out.

I turn to the kids and clap my hands. "So, who's ready to make some pizza?" Quinn and Elle shout that they're ready, and I spy Peyton looking away. I can't force her, but I'm going to try. "Okay, Quinn, take Elle into the kitchen and get the stuff out to make pizza. I want to talk to Peyton a little bit."

I watch until they disappear around the corner. Quinn has made pizzas with me many times so he can at least pull out everything we need. I move toward Peyton and climb the steps until I'm about three away from her.

"I know we don't know each other very well, but I thought maybe you could help me make the pizza crust. I always end up being a hand short and since I only have two and need an extra, would you mind helping?"

Peyton turns slightly and runs her finger along the wood grain on the step. I take her silence as a giant no.

"Well, if you change your mind, we'll be in the kitchen."

I have no choice but to leave her. She has to come around on her own. I know that if I force her, she'll never become my friend.

Quinn has the flour and yeast out, along with a large mixing bowl. He's a pro and can probably make the dough with his eyes closed.

"Do you guys make your own pizza?" I ask, as I slip an apron on.

"We tried, but Mom isn't very good at it." Quinn says, causing my heart to skip a beat. So many times we wanted him to say the word 'Mom' to someone and be able to mean it. Lord knows his biological mother is a lost cause.

We work as a team making dough, mixing sauce, slicing pepperoni and grating the cheese. Quinn is a little chef, and Elle is eager to learn. Every few minutes I check on Peyton, and every so often she's moved down a step. Quinn makes sure to make her a pizza just the way she likes it, and I marvel at how well he's adjusted to having siblings.

I'm pleasantly surprised when Peyton decides to join us at the dinner table. We eat in silence minus the praises of how good their pizzas have turned out.

"So, do you want your mom and dad to have another baby?" Three pairs of eyes find mine and if I didn't know better, I'd think I'm in one of those horror movies where the children slice up the babysitter.

"No!" all three reply in unison before they go back to eating. I make a mental note to ask Katelyn their plans because if a baby is in the future, they might want to try family counseling first.

I tell the kids not to worry about the dishes, and for them to go change and meet me in the family room. I microwave a few bags of popcorn and dump it into two bowls. The family room is probably the coziest place in the house. A large sectional couch takes up most of the space, with beanbag chairs spread around. They have a huge television, which takes up half the wall. All three of them come down in their pajamas, carrying blankets.

With the movie in, I sit down only to have Quinn crawl up and snuggle in next to me. He's my best bud, and I've missed him. He makes me want to move closer, but I'm just not sure I can. The girls chose the first movie, some *Disney* musical. Quinn balks at first, but it doesn't take him long to start singing along.

The loud knock on the door scares all of us. The girls let out a yelp, and my heart starts thrashing in my throat. Quinn runs to the door before I can stop him. I get there just as he opens it and find Xander, the incredibly good-looking trainer with the I-want-to-bend-you-over-my weight-bench-and-have-my-way-with-you eyes. I swallow hard when he realizes that I'm checking him out. Shoot me for staring, but I'm a female who can appreciate the fine art of a good-looking man.

"Hey, uh… is Harrison here?"

"He's out with my mom," Quinn answers before I can say anything.

"She's my mom, too," Elle adds as she comes up behind us.

Quinn rolls his eyes and corrects himself. "Our mom."

"Oh… all right."

"Wanna come in?" Quinn is asking before I can even get a single syllable formed in my head.

"Um…" Xander looks over his shoulder, and I can't help but look, too. Does he have someone in his car? I can't see anyone and when he turns back around, our eyes meet, and I find it hard to look away. When we were in the gym this morning, I tried to ignore what my body was telling me. He's a professional, and today I was his client. But now my body is screaming at me, telling me to appreciate the man in front of me. I'm staring. I'm taking in his well-defined arms and allowing my eyes to trace the intricate art that makes up his full sleeve. My stomach decides to tie itself into intricate knots; increasing the welcomed anxiety I haven't felt since the first day I met Oliver. Xander is taller, broader than what I'm used to. His dark hair is kept short but styled. His eyes are as blue as the ocean, and I can see myself staring into them for hours.

I shake my head to clear my thoughts and end up laughing. He looks at me with his eyebrow raised. I'm such a fool.

"Please come in," I say, knowing that I'm going to regret this moment for the rest of my life.

Quinn opens the door wider to allow Xander to step in and slams it shut immediately. The kids run back to the family room and Xander follows. His cologne is strong and overtaking my senses. I try not to let it affect me, but the truth of the matter is, it does. Maybe this is my wake-up call solidifying the fact that my decision to part ways with Oliver was the correct one.

Xander sits at the opposite end of the couch and my evil spawn of a nephew decides that he wants to sit on the floor.

"Sorry about the movie choice," I offer, in the lamest

attempt at conversation ever.

"It's fine, I've seen this a few times." And to prove his point he breaks out in his own rendition of *Let it Go*, which causes the twins to start laughing. I laugh as well and end up busting out what must be the loudest snort in the history of snorts.

I can fade away now and die from embarrassment.

"What was that?" he asks, laughing.

Of course he heard it.

I whip my head, refusing to answer, and in doing so I pinch a nerve in my neck. "Ouch," I say as I start rubbing my neck. I woke up with a stiff neck but figured it was from traveling and sleeping an unfamiliar bed.

"Here, let me." Before I can say anything, Xander has me pulled in front of him, his fingers expertly kneading the spot I was rubbing.

"Oh god, that feels so good," I mumble. I'm in heaven, lost under the tenderness of this touch. This man has magic hands and my mind instantly goes south thinking about the other parts of me he could massage. The way his fingers dig into the right spot without causing too much pain amazes me. He leans in a little closer, his chest pressing to my back. His breath tickles my neck, causing the fine hairs to rise. I squeeze my legs together to fight off the impending ache. I shouldn't feel like this, but I do. Every part of me is beginning to tingle because this hot-as-sin man is touching me.

"Auntie, we're going to bed." My eyes fling open and I stand, moving away from Xander. Quinn, Peyton and Elle are all smiling at me with their arms full of their blankets.

"I'll take you."

"We're good." They say as run off and start stomping up the stairs laughing.

"Little shits," I mumble, as I walk over to the television. The movie isn't over, yet they sure were in a hurry to get to bed.

"I should go." I turn as Xander stands, putting us chest to chest. Our hands are down by our sides, only centimeters apart. It would take one flick of the wrist, and I could brush my finger along his. If I inhale, my chest will brush against his. I take a chance and look up. He's staring down at me, his eyes blazing with heat. The attraction is there.

I step away. "Would you like some wine?" I ask, before mentally kicking my own ass. Wine is the last thing we need right now.

"I'd love some."

Me too. The whole damn bottle so I can forget this moment. Xander follows me into the kitchen and sees our mess from earlier. I ignore it. We'll have one glass, and he'll leave. That'll be the end of whatever *this* is.

I pull out the bottle, and he takes it from me, popping the cork like a pro. I take two glasses out of the cabinet and hand them to him. He pours for both of us, and picks up the wine filled glasses, carrying them over to the table. The very same table that has our half-eaten pizza mess all over it.

"Sorry about the mess. I was going to clean it after the movie, and now after this glass." I hold up my glass to him before brining it to my lips.

"I'll help."

I shake my head. "You will not. You didn't make the mess."

Xander shrugs and takes a sip. "Tell me about yourself, Yvie."

I look at him, and raise my eyebrow. "Can't say much has changed from earlier."

Xander blushes, and I decide right then and there that is one of the hottest things I've ever seen a man do. "I want to know about you, not my client who was telling me her ass is too big. And for the record, it's not."

"I know, you said that earlier."

"I meant it."

I sit up a bit straighter and lean in. I can't hide my attraction for him even if I wanted to. "I'm four years younger than my brother. I'm here to get to know his family. I'm a dancer. And I think that's it. Now tell me about you."

"I was hired by Liam to care for JD. I quickly became the band's personal trainer and opened my own gym a few months ago. I'm single, never married and I have no children or any loose ends."

The last bit of information makes me pause. Why is he telling me this?

"I'm single, never married and I don't have children unless you count my nephew and two nieces."

He nods. "Well, yes, I think we can both count them. I do spend my fair share of time with them."

"I love them. I miss Quinn and really need to get to know Peyton and Elle better. Getting pictures on my phone doesn't do them justice. It doesn't even compare to seeing them."

"You know, your pictures don't do you justice."

The wine must be talking. He wouldn't be saying this to me if he were sober.

"Katelyn's description of you didn't do you justice either." Yes, definitely the wine talking. I bring my glass to my lips and notice that it's full again. I can't help but take a drink without removing my eyes from him. I close my eyes and shake my head only to open them again to find him looking at me. He doesn't let go while he holds my gaze.

He studies me for what seems like an eternity. I'm not sure if I like that I'm under this microscope or not, but one thing I like for sure is that he's interested. I catch myself looking from his eyes to his lips and before I know it I'm leaning in, and he's leaning in and we're inches apart.

I pull away and down the rest of my wine. "I need to clean." I rush to the sink and start filling it with hot water and probably too much soap. I watch as the soapsuds build into a high tower before I shut off the water. Before I can move, Xander is right behind me, his arms on either side of me and goosebumps rise on the back of my neck from his close proximity. I should feel like he's invading my personal space, but I don't. I welcome the wispy warmth of his breath blowing softly on my neck, and I'm fighting the urge to lean back onto his broad chest. He picks up a plate and drops it into the water. Suds fly everywhere and a few land on my face, hitting my nose and lips. I blow them away, but to no avail. I start to laugh and turn around to look at him.

His face is one of happiness. His eyes are sparkling and it makes me wonder what someone has to do to gain that sort of euphoria in life where the simplest little things make you happy. Harrison has it in his life. I want it in mine.

Xander cups my face. My hands immediately find his wrist, and I hang on for what I suspect will be the most amazing kiss ever. His head turns slightly and his nose brushes against mine, not once, not twice, but three times. I lick my lips in anticipation.

"I think I got it," he says, pulling away.

"What?" I squeak out.

"The soap suds on your nose. I got them."

I'm dumbfounded as he backs out of the kitchen

without taking his eyes off of me.

"See ya later, Yvie," he says before I'm able to comprehend what the hell just happened. The front door shuts, bringing me back to reality. He totally just played me for a fool, making me believe that the feeling was mutual and that we were on the verge of the kiss to end all kisses. That jerk got me worked up and ditched out.

Revenge will be mine.

CHAPTER 6
XANDER

MEMBERSHIP has increased at the gym, mostly women from neighboring towns. For the most part, it's obvious as to why they joined this gym and not one near their homes. It used to bother me until Liam told me to capitalize on it, saying he said he didn't care and that it was good for business. Harrison is impartial, and JD likes the attention. In fact, I think he, out of the three of them, gets a total kick out of flirting with the women here. I've told him to be kind, that they're likely to get hurt when he winks at them, but he doesn't listen. You'd never know he's happily married with a year-old baby at home. He's all talk and no action.

Hell, action is what I wanted last night, and I have a feeling Yvie would've been a willing player. But I'm not like that, and I shouldn't be with her. Even if she weren't Harrison's sister, she's only here for a week or so and the last thing I want is to start a relationship with someone who lives in a different state. Long distance love affairs and a business like mine just don't mix. If I allowed myself to, I can see myself being very attached to Yvie. She has some of the qualities that I look for in a woman: she takes care of her body, she's funny, sexy and can hold my attention fully. She's a dangerous combination for me right now, and it's probably best that I keep my distance, keep our budding relationship strictly professional.

I have a feeling that keeping my distance is going to be an issue though. Yvie is going to be at every party and every function I attend in the next few days. I could just stay home. Avoidance has worked in the past. Except, I won't have a valid excuse when the guys, or even wives, come calling to ask why I'm not there. I've been invited, I've RSVP'd and it's not like I have all these offers from people asking me to share the holidays with them.

Staying out of Katelyn's kitchen is a must though. Memories from last night are very present and each time I start to think about Yvie, I can see her caged against the counter with soap suds on her nose, her chest rising and falling with every breath she takes as her eyes pierce into mine, her pink tongue wetting her lips in anticipation. All I had to do was let my head fall and she would've caught me. I could be sitting here blissed out from kissing her. Instead, I'm in the gym sporting a freaking semi and there isn't jack shit I can do it about it because as far as I'm concerned Yvie James is off limits.

I busy myself behind the computer instead of mingling with the patrons. The counter provides for great coverage of my issue but does nothing to keep my mind from wandering back to last night. I should've told Quinn "no thanks" when he invited me in, and I should've left as soon as they went to bed. Oh, and the massage definitely shouldn't have happened, but I couldn't resist the pull to touch her. I had to curb my appetite from earlier. Watching her work on her glutes, a section of her body that doesn't need work, drove me nuts, and I had no reason to touch her.

Last night she gave me every reason in the world, and I started to take advantage. I didn't want to stop, but it wasn't the time or the place to explore my ballerina… my what? She can't be my anything.

"What's up, mate? You look bloody knackered. Did your willy keep you busy last night?" I look up to find JD resting on the counter with a shit-eating grin on his face. Being friends with JD means you can't take him seriously. At least not all the time because he likes to joke. And by joke, I mean make crude comments at the most inopportune time. That's what makes him unique.

"Morning, JD," I say, without acknowledging the rest of his statement.

"A mate who avoids another mate's question is a surefire way of telling said mate that he got a little last night."

"He better not have, unless it was after he left my house." As soon as Harrison finishes that sentence, I look away as my body temperature changes. I hate that I blush like a little boy. My mom assured me I'd outgrow it, but it's gotten worse. It's a sign of embarrassment and the last thing I need is for Harrison to catch on that I want to see his sister naked. Not even see her naked, but touch her while she's naked. I'm all sorts of messed up right now.

"Oh, bloody hell, you stuck your willy in Yvie?"

With the addition of Liam, six eyes now glare at me. If blushing wasn't telling them something, the fact that I'm tongue-tied is. I clear my throat and stand, thinking about old ladies in granny panties batting their eyes at me without their dentures in, anything to get the semi to go away. Today, gym shorts are not my friend.

"Do you guys want to work out or stand around gossiping like girls?" I ask, as I walk past them.

"I'm more interested in finding out what went on with you and my sister last night. When we came home, she went straight to bed, but failed to explain why there were soap suds in the sink and random soap stains on the countertop and floor."

"I want to know what he's doing with Yvie to begin with," Liam adds in a brotherly I'm-going-to-kick-your-ass-for-looking-at-my-sister tone.

My problem is, if I look at them, they'll see through me. Avoiding eye contact is what I need to do. "I left when she started doing the dishes," I say, as I pick up the weight and slide it onto the dumbbell for Liam. Of all the guys, he's the most serious about weight training. It's something he kept up from his football days. He's probably the buffest lead singer out there, and he drives the women crazy when he flexes. I know this because Josie likes to gossip about her husband.

"Did the dishes get done, Harrison?"

I look at the three of them behind me. Harrison shrugs but smiles. JD is grinning from ear to ear, and Liam looks pissed. Always the leader of the gang, Liam is. I shake my head, hoping to convey that nothing happened and nothing will.

"Liam, you're up." He takes the bench and lies under the bar. I assist him, lifting the bar and watching as he moves the dumbbell up and down with ease. Harrison is just a few steps away using the hand weights, and JD is on the treadmill. JD isn't keen on lifting weights; he doesn't want to ruin his figure he says. Harrison does mostly arms, and he and I run at night. Liam is my main focus.

"So you and Yvie, huh?" he asks as he sets the

dumbbell on the bar catchers. He sits up and loosens his arms while I add more weight.

"I just met her yesterday," I tell him, as he lies back down for his next set.

"She has a douche for a boyfriend," Liam adds, throwing me back a little. She never mentioned a boyfriend and had plenty of time to say something. That is just another reason for her and me to steer clear of each other.

"She broke up with him," Harrison says, shooting down my most recent reason to stay away. "She's never been serious about him anyway."

"You should hit that," JD says, appearing out of nowhere.

I step back and put my hands up. "Hold on here, guys. First off, she's your sister." I point at Harrison who shrugs. "Secondly, I'm not hitting anything." JD grins. "And third, shouldn't Harrison be the one giving me the third degree?" Liam doesn't say anything because he's too busy pushing the dumbbell back into place. "I just met her. She's pretty, but give me a break, guys. I'm trying to be respectful here."

"So you admit that you think Yvie is hot?" JD says, raising his eyebrows.

I throw my hands up and walk away, letting them finish their workout.

"At least we know he can count to three," Liam says, causing the other two to start laughing. I give them the bird as I disappear into my office.

I'm not in my office thirty seconds when Harrison pokes his head in. "You had to know it was coming."

"Nothing happened, I swear."

"It can. I mean, if you wanted it to and she was game. I'm not *that* big brother, in case you're wondering. I mean,

I'd kill you if you hurt her, but she's an adult and can make her own choices. Just be sure to wrap your dick." He shuts the door before I can even respond.

I bang my head on my desk in quick succession. I feel like I'm back in high school stuck in the locker room after watching the cheerleaders practice. Every guy got a stiffy for them, especially our freshman year, except she's not a cheerleader. She's a ballerina with a smoking hot body, killer eyes and thinking about her makes me hard. I can't even consider the fact that she's one of my best friends' sister. The only thing that matters is that she's leaving, and I'm not into long distance romances, Skyping and waiting in overcrowded airports. I want the real thing, in living color.

After the last gym member leaves, I shut off the lights. All this week I've let my staff leave early so they can finish their Christmas shopping or prepare their holiday meals. My mom used to start baking the week before Christmas so I know what it's like. I didn't cut any hours; everyone has been working during the day, which has proved beneficial since the gym is spotless, all the equipment is cleaned and we're fully stocked for the New Year.

The chime on the door signals, telling me that someone has just walked in. It would've made sense that I locked the door when I turned off the lights, but any sense I had today has been living in my nether region.

"We're closed," I yell out as I walk around the corner. I stop dead in my tracks when I see Yvie standing in the middle of the gym glowing like an angel thanks to the street lights shining in from outside. She's carrying a plate in her hands and is looking everywhere but at me.

"I didn't realize you closed so early."

I shrug and take a few steps toward her. The smell of brownies, cookies and all-round goodness meets my senses, reminding me that it's been years since I've had someone bake for me.

"I thought people needed time to shop and didn't want them to feel guilty that they hadn't worked out so I'm closing early this week."

Yvie nods and continues to look past me. "These are for you. The kids and I were baking and I thought… I don't know, it's probably stupid. I don't really eat sweet things because I'm always watching my weight –"

"You don't need to." That statement gets her attention, and her eyes meet mine. There's a small hint of a smile, but it quickly fades. This woman has been damaged, and it makes me see red. No man, regardless of his position, should ever tell a woman she's fat. Curves or no curves, women are beautiful.

Yvie walks to the counter and sets down the plate. I'm tempted to rush over, snatch it from her hands and rip it off the cover. I have a feeling she's a damn good cook in the kitchen, which is one reason she worries so much about keeping her weight down.

"I should probably go. I have to find a place to practice. I thought I could convince myself I need a vacation, but I find myself *needing* to go through my routine." Yvie looks away and sighs. "I'm sorry, you didn't need to hear me ramble. I'll let you finish closing up.

"Wait," I say, reaching out to stop her. Our hands touch and the hairs on my arm stand. My skin instantly feels clammy, and if I didn't know any better I'd think I'm sick, but that's not the case right now.

"You can practice here. I have the mirrors and can move some of the equipment to give you space."

I don't give her a chance to tell me no. I set off and start moving as much as I can without assistance. I'm by no means a weight lifter, but the adrenaline pumping through me right now is giving me enough force to move mountains.

Sweat beads form on my forehead and neck. I pull my shirt off and wipe my face, neck and back. Her gasp freezes my actions. I pull my shirt away slowly and drop it to the floor. The air in the room is thick, laden with tension still left over from last night. I turn away, breaking our concentration on each other, reminding myself that not only is she Harrison's sister, but she's just passing through.

I turn on the sound system, and change the station to something softer. When I turn toward the space I just cleared, Yvie is standing in front of the mirror in nothing but a sports bar and some very tight shorts. The pants and sweatshirt she was wearing earlier are long forgotten. She's barefoot and her legs are slightly spread apart. Her head rolls as her shoulders shrug, loosening up her muscles.

Yvie starts moving to the music with a tremendous amount of grace and elegance. I've never paid much attention to any type of dancer before, and I'm quickly realizing that this is the finest form of art I've ever seen. Walking to the weight bench, I sit down and watch. Yvie is in a trance and doesn't know I'm even in the room. Her eyes are focused on the mirror as she watches me watch her. I've never been so turned on in my life. A private dance meant just for me.

Her hips swivel to the music as her hands find her hair. I'm jealous of the mirror for getting the show it is. I swallow hard when her hand rubs over her bra-clad breast and her chest rises. I want to be the one to elicit that movement from her.

I close my eyes and chide myself for getting hard from watching her. She's working, I'm just an ignorant observer, but my body thinks otherwise. It wants her. I want her. From the moment she walked into my gym with Katelyn, she turned me on and watching her now is doing nothing to curb my appetite for her. It's only whetting it, making it stronger.

My eyes spring open when weight is added to my lap. She's straddling me, rocking against me. My hands grip her hips pushing her back and forth, faster. Yvie's hands pull at my hair, tilting my neck to the side. Her teeth graze my earlobe causing me to hiss. This is by far the most erotic out-of-body moment I've ever experienced.

"Can I touch you?" I beg her with my voice. Her answer is to pinch my nipple, causing my cock to react even more. I slide the strap of her sport bra over her shoulder, pulling it down just below the most perfect set of breasts I have ever been graced with. The bra settles underneath, pulling them closer and leaving her tits on perfect display. Her right one is in my mouth, as my hand massages and tweaks her left. I alternate quickly, lapping and sucking her taut nipples.

Yvie scoots back, cutting me off from having my fantasy play out. Every man has dreamt of having sex in a gym. I knew this was too good to be true. That is until she stands and shimmies out of her ballet shorts. She stands before me partially naked and perfect. I look into her eyes, shining and alight with passion. I stand and awkwardly try to remove my shorts and boxers as fast as possible. She walks toward me, pushing me back onto the bench. I swallow hard as my hands come into contact with her outstanding ass. I squeeze her gently, pulling her forward as her hand wraps around my rigid cock.

I'm used to being in control when it comes to sex, but this woman is taking whatever it is that she needs from me, and I'm willing to give her everything if it means I get to experience her for a brief moment.

Yvie straddles and guides me to where she needs me the most. Maybe this is what she needs, someone who can appreciate her magnificent body. If that's the case, I can do this all night long.

My eyes roll back and Yvie sits on me, enveloping me in her sweet-as-sin pussy. She places her hands on my chest, pushing me to lie back. I hiss as she moves up and down, using the weight bar for leverage. Her breasts bounce, asking me to hold them, and I do.

I sit up, unable to take it anymore. I need to feel her body against mine, but she's not having it. She leans back, placing her hands behind her on the bench, her flexibility paying off in spades. My eyes leave hers and travel to where we're connected. To where she's riding my cock. It's the hottest fucking thing I've ever witnessed or been a part of. I reach down and rub my thumb over her clit and watch as her head falls back. Yvie moans, sending shock waves to my dick. The urgency to come is there. I grab her hips, increasing the tempo.

I scream out when her walls start squeezing the shit out of my cock and for the first time, she kisses me. Her lips are hard against mine, her tongue dominating. I forget everything as I hold the back of her head, unwilling to let this kiss end. I jerk once, twice, as I empty into her. She knows that she's won this battle. Her hips slow down and she slowly moves off of me. I look at her, but she looks away, her lower lip between her teeth.

Reaching out, I pull it out and place a soft kiss there before getting up. My shorts are tangled around just one ankle and I try to step into them without falling on my face.

"Let me go grab something to clean up," I say before disappearing into the locker room. It was stupid to say, but thanking her for rocking my world seemed worse.

When I come back into the gym, she's not on the bench. In fact, she's nowhere to be seen. Her coat, clothes and shoes are gone.

She's left.

CHAPTER 7
YVIE

'VE never been a last-minute shopper until this year. Now I'm shoulder to shoulder with angry women fighting for the very last game console that every child needs this year. I've never waited this long, and as I walk through the crowded mall, I can't help but think I knew subconsciously that I wouldn't be in New York this Christmas because, by my calculations, I should've had this all done and shipped out here to Beaumont.

I also hate shopping by myself. Even though Katelyn and I bought some presents a few days ago, there are still a few more gifts that I need to buy. Katelyn had to fill in for Josie because she's not feeling great. Katelyn is hoping that's it's morning sickness and that Josie and Liam are finally expanding their family. According to Katelyn, they're trying and have been since before they married almost two years ago but they still haven't conceived. She says that Josie is starting to freak out.

I don't blame her though. I think that when a woman wants a child, it's all she thinks about. After the other night, it's what I should be thinking about. We didn't use protection and while I was there, experiencing him that way, I couldn't have cared less. I just wanted what he was offering. I was so stupid for going to the gym to confront Xander. Everything I had planned to say went out the door as soon as I saw him. My brother was likely trying to get under my skin when he started teasing me about their earlier conversation, and he succeeded. Just not the way he thought. It pissed me off that Xander would discuss me with the guys while they worked out.

The night he showed up, I was nervous. I hadn't eaten that much with the kids and after the little instigators ditched me and the wine came out, I couldn't suck it down fast enough. Just looking at Xander makes me want to forget my life in New York.

What I did at the gym – I've never done anything like that. It was raw and pure. Being with Xander like that made me feel like a woman who could conquer the world. I hate that I left without saying goodbye. I just couldn't face him after what we did. To say I'm physically attracted to Xander would be an epic understatement. Not only do I have Katelyn reminding me of how hot he is, but the way he carries himself shows me that he's one hundred percent pure man. And I thought I could keep up my wall and not let anyone chip away at it. I was so wrong.

Oliver isn't anything like Xander when it comes to sex. Oliver is boring – I guess it's how I'd describe him after what I experienced last night. Lights off, only in a bed and always at night. Maybe it's age, or maybe it's me. And maybe Xander is just a better lover or maybe Oliver thinks I'm the one who's boring.

No, Xander isn't a lover, at least not to me. He probably

thinks of me as a slut for what I did last night. Going there with a plate of food as my excuse to see him was wrong. It was like an out-of-body experience, except I enjoyed every tantalizing moment. I welcomed every touch, and every caress. I begged for him to grab my hips and pull me roughly against him. And when I kissed him – that's when I knew I couldn't stay there. I would've ended up in his bed and never left. He made me feel like Julia Roberts in *Pretty Woman* — minus the paid-for sex part.

The sex was... like nothing I had ever experienced before. It was sensual and erotic and all consuming. It was everything and nothing I thought a random hook-up would be. Xander could've taken control at any time, but he let me lead the way. He was patient and willing to submit to my desires. From the moment he took his shirt off, I knew that I was going to do whatever I could to get close to him. I wanted to touch him. I wanted to be the one who wiped the sweat away from his torso. I wanted to be able to feel his muscles flex because of my touch. Watching him in the mirror as I danced made my body tingle with anticipation of what he and I could be together. I wanted to know what he felt like against my body. If I could play that on rewind, I would. Just remembering that moment is enough to have me running back to his gym just to stare at the piece of furniture that withstood everything he was giving me.

I sit down in the center of the mall and people watch. From my vantage point, I have a clear view of the candy store, the mall Santa Claus, a hat store, plus all the kiosks that clog up the open mall space during the holidays. My fingers crumple the piece of paper in my jacket pocket. It's my Christmas list and there are only two things on there: one for Harrison and the other for Quinn. I'm at a loss as to what I should buy for the twins or Katelyn. Fact of the matter is, I don't know them well enough to shop for them. If I were still in New York, I'd probably send something from *FAO Schwartz* for the twins, but I'm here and I'll be watching them open their gifts on Christmas morning. Impression is everything.

Buying for Katelyn shouldn't be too bad, but it is. My brother spoils her, dotes on her. She mentions that she likes something and it's in the house the next day. When he does stuff like that it makes it hard for my mom and me to buy her something special. And that's my conundrum – what do I buy three of the most important people in my brother's life for Christmas?

I sigh heavily as two ladies walk by. They give me a dirty look and for the life of me I can't understand why. Do they not feel the holiday pressure? Maybe this is telling me that I'm not cut out for family life, that being single and living in an apartment in one of the busiest cities is all that I'm meant for.

I remove the tattered piece of paper from my pocket and roll it into a ball. I unroll and roll again just out of frustration.

"What did that paper do to you?" Xander's voice startles me, and instantly my heart starts racing and my body takes me back to the gym... the weight bench... and his hands gripping my hips. He'll never know this, but he left bruises. He marked me, and I enjoyed it.

He sits down next to me and rests his elbows on his legs. He turns and looks at me. I can't maintain eye contact because I'm embarrassed about what we did, about what I did and how I left things. We hold each other's gazes until I have to look away. I'm afraid if I stare at him too long, I'll see something that might scare me, like the truth about our one night stand.

"I'm glad I ran into you," he says.

"Oh yeah, why's that?" I can't imagine why he wants to even talk to me.

"I don't like the way things were left the other night. That's not who I am, and I'm pretty sure that wasn't you either."

I scoff. "It was me, I was there." I play it off like our night together was no big deal. I don't want him to see through me, to see the anguish I'm dealing with. The thought of him telling me to leave or him thanking me are other factors in me bailing as soon as he went to the bathroom.

He sits up, and shakes his head. "I'm not talking about *that*, I'm talking about how things were when you left."

I turn slightly to face Xander and wish I hadn't. Seeing him here like this and sitting next to me makes me wish the other night didn't happen. But it did and now I have to pay the price. "Look, I'm sorry about last night. It never should've happened. I put you in a horrible situation, and that's wrong. I can understand if you don't want to be friends and avoid me like the plague until I'm gone. I promise not to make the holidays uncomfortable for you. I'll be out of town in no time."

Xander's lips go into a thin line as he shakes his head. Disappointment masks his features. Who knew coming clean about being a psycho was a bad thing?

"Sometimes I think you talk too much. I don't regret the other night. Yes, there are some things I'd like to change, but being with you, like that… I've never felt so out of control and completely calm in my life. You're like this pint-sized hurricane that's rolling through town, and I'm the weather man chasing the storm. I'm not gonna lie, last night was amazing — different, but worth it. You're like a fantasy come true."

Xander pauses and watches the shoppers. There's

a group of young kids, a few with their arms around each other that seem to be having a good time. They're laughing and carrying on. One of the guys is even holding his girlfriend's shopping bags.

"I think you and I got off on the wrong foot, and so what if we did things a little backwards? You're here for a week or so and need to have a good time. It just so happens that I'm available if you're interested."

Xander juts out his arm, giving my hand a resting place if I chose to accept.

"One condition," I say, putting the power back into my hands.

"What's that?"

"That you don't tell my brother, Liam or Jimmy what happened."

Xander laughs that stupid guy laugh where he's not sure if he's been caught or if he's heard something stupid. He picks up my hand and places his lips there in one of the sweetest moments of my life.

"I'd never tell your brother, or anyone else for that matter, about us. That's between us, and only us. I know the guys gossip like women, but I'm still on the outside. And even though I have your brother's blessing, I think I'd rather keep our escapades between us."

"Excuse me, what?" I ask, confused as to why he was asking Harrison for his blessing. "You asked my brother?"

Xander puts his hands up. "It's not what you're thinking. He came to me, and said he wouldn't have a problem if we dated."

"Oh," I say, immediately feeling stupid. "That's just… I don't have a dad, ya know? He died when I was a baby and Harrison has always been the man of the house. So, wow I guess he approves of you." I try and force a smile, but fail miserably. Xander pulls me into his arms, and I use this to my advantage to smell his cologne. He smells like home. I know it sounds odd, but it's the best way to describe it. I feel at ease in his arms.

"I'm sorry about your dad; Harrison never mentioned it. And for the record, I'm happy he gave me permission because I'd like to spend as much time with you as possible until you leave."

I pull away and wipe under my eyes. I'm not crying, but my eyes are misty. "I think I'd like that too. It sucks being the fifth wheel."

Xander laughs, and it's the most beautiful sound I've heard in a long time. "You have no idea."

CHAPTER 8
XANDER

BUMPING into Yvie at the mall was not by mistake. Quinn is quite the little matchmaker when he wants to be. I know it's wrong asking a child for dirt on his aunt, but desperate times call for desperate measures. I needed to see her, so I went to Harrison's. She wasn't there, but Quinn was all too forthcoming with the fact that she left to go shopping. Fate was on my side when I walked in and there she was, sitting in the "man" section as Liam calls it.

I stood there, watching her for a few minutes before approaching. Truth be told, I was working up the nerve to face her. What she and I did last night was every fantasy I've ever had, but I never thought it would play out like that. Now every time I close my eyes, I see her in the mirror begging me with her eyes. My gym will never be the same after last night. Her body is nothing like the women I see coming in and out of the gym. Her long legs and dancer body are a turn on, and I didn't know that's what I'd be attracted to until I saw her.

Sitting next to her, I find myself wanting to take her back to my house. Not for sex, although I wouldn't rule that out, but just to be with her in private. To hold her, to be the shoulder she leans into when the movie we're watching is too sad or she's scared. I find myself wanting to cook her dinner and massage her feet after a long day of rehearsals. The latter is a long-term dream that I don't foresee happening. I shouldn't even be thinking past the end of the week. She's not staying here.

The urge to hold her hand is strong, but I resist. I think she needs a friend, not some horny ass man trying to get in her pants. Besides, Harrison mentioned that her producer used to be her boyfriend. I don't want to think that the other night was a rebound fuck, but the thought has been plaguing my mind.

Thing is, I can see Yvie as someone with whom to settle down. The only problem in my thought process is that she's a big city girl who doesn't need small town life. It has nothing to offer her and frankly, neither do I. When you're someone like Yvie James – performing on Broadway – the last thing that looks appealing is a gym owner.

My problem is that I overthink everything. Yvie and I are both adults and capable of making our own decisions. I could go down the friends' route and just hang out with her while she's here, or I can break my own heart and put it all out there for her. The third option is to do both. Take whatever this connection is between us and make the best of it, and if that means we end up naked and on my weight bench with her legs straddling me, so be it. I'll just be there when she gets on the plane and heads back to New York City.

I take her hand in mine and start walking. She has a list of presents to buy and if it means I get to spend the day with her, I'm going to brave the crowds.

"Who do you have left to buy for?" I ask her as we meander through the hoards of people.

"The twins," she says as she lets out a sigh. I can't tell if it's from frustration or if she's just being dramatic.

I laugh, hoping to put her at ease. "Is that a good thing?"

"No, it's not. I don't know them very well so I'm really not sure what to buy them. With Quinn, it's easy. With Peyton and Elle, not so much."

One of the benefits of living in Beaumont is going to be my savior. "I can help, you know, if you want me to? I've spent some time with them and know what they like."

Yvie stops us, much to the disgruntled shoppers who have to move around us. "Am I a bad aunt for not spending more time with them?"

I move us to the side so we aren't bumped and pushed by others. "Many people live away from their relatives. You can't think that you're a bad aunt because you don't know what the girls like. Quinn grew up with you and the twins have only just come into your life. You need time to get to know them."

"I know, but how do I do that living in New York?"

"Tell Harrison that he has to bring the kids to you for at least a month every summer," I say with a smirk. Her face lights up acknowledging that I am a genius. "C'mon, twinkle toes, let's get this shopping done." I put my arm around her shoulders and pull her into me. It'd be so easy to capture her lips, but I refrain. I opt for the ever platonic kiss on the forehead and call it good.

Within two steps of entering the holiday foot traffic, my hand drops from her shoulder, my fingers entwining with hers. It's more intimate, at least for me. I direct Yvie to a very girly store. I've seen these bags litter the James' house so I know one of the girls likes to shop here. My guess is Elle. She's the princess in the making, always trying to steal the spotlight. It's not hard with how shy Peyton is, and without a doubt Quinn is her protector. I've been around enough to watch him with her. He's always in front, guarding her from whatever may come her way.

"I think a bottle of Pepto Bismol exploded in this store," Yvie says, as soon as we step in. She's right; it's very pink.

"This is Elle's favorite store."

Yvie nods and starts looking around. I hang back, waiting to see what she picks out. I bought the kids a couple of board games. As much as they include me, I still feel like I'm on the outside a little. They've all known each other for years and are a family through and through. I'm just thankful they invite me to be a part of their lives.

"What do you think of this?"

"Um, what is that?" All I see is something pink, short and lots of ruffles.

"It's a tutu, but one that Elle could wear to school."

I shrug. "You're the woman here. All I can tell you is that she's very girly."

Yvie bites her lip and nods, and I find myself wanting to rub her lower lip and kiss away the pain she's causing it. I have to stop thinking like this. The last thing I want to do is confuse her about my feelings. Hell, I don't want to confuse myself about my feelings. The ones I'm having now are causing me enough grief.

I take the bag from Yvie as soon as she's done paying. She looks at me and smiles, holding my gaze as she slips her hand back into mine. I could definitely get used to having her around, which tells me I need to put up a wall and shut off all emotions. She's leaving, and I know I'm not enough to keep her here. Not that I'd even try. She's a big city girl with big city dreams. She needs to fulfill those dreams in order to be happy.

"Peyton's next," she says as we walk back into the mall. I direct us toward the large department store. This will give Yvie the opportunity to choose from various items. She could go with something sporty, buy Peyton a game, or go with the safe option and pick out clothes.

"I know she likes football, but what else?"

"Well, sometimes she dresses like her sister, but only when Katelyn makes her for photos. She likes music, and plays Harrison's drums all the time. She likes to hang out with Noah and Liam on weekends because they watch a lot of football. When you think about it, she's a very well-rounded little girl."

Yvie sighs as she starts look through racks of clothes. "I don't think she likes me."

I lean onto the rack to catch her attention. "She doesn't know you. From what Harrison has said, she's afraid that if she loves someone they'll leave her. It took her a while to cozy up to Harrison and now she doesn't let him out of her sight unless she's with Liam; and if Quinn and Noah are around, you can forget existing. They create a bubble for her that even Elle isn't a part of."

"Interesting," she states as she walks out of this section. I try not to smile when she waits for me, holding out her hand. She's never going to know this, but this gesture alone makes me feel like I'm on top of world.

We spend an hour in this store until Yvie is satisfied with what's she's picked for Peyton: a set of pajamas and a necklace with a football charm. Yvie says she's catering to both the girl and tomboy sides.

As soon as we're in the parking lot, I walk Yvie to my car and put her bags in there quickly before she can balk. I take her hand again and pull her back toward the mall.

"Where are we going?"

"I have a surprise."

If I'm not mistaken, there might be a slight smile creeping over her face. I'm trying to keep my eyes facing forward, but I'm definitely sneaking glances at her.

I open the door to the ice skating rink and hear a slight gasp from her. She turns, and places her arms around my waist.

"How'd you know I love ice skating?"

"I didn't, but am surely thanking my quick thinking for bringing you here."

After paying the rental fee, we both hurry to get our skates on. Holding her hand, we step out onto the ice and start gliding. Yvie lets go of my hand and skates away. She turns to face me, skating backwards like a pro.

"Wow, and here I thought I'd get to hold your hand the entire time," I say as she circles me.

"I try to do this once a week. Oliver doesn't like it, but I don't care."

"Your ex?" I ask, quickly regretting my question. Harrison told his name in confidence and my big mouth likely just ruined everything.

Yvie slows down in front of me, setting her hands on my chest to stop me. "He's my producer, and yes, he's also my ex. I broke up with him because I'm not sure about my life right now. He wants one thing, and I'm not sure I want that with him. I also want to make it on my own. I don't want to get a lead because of who my boyfriend is, ya know?"

No, not really. "Yeah, I get it."

"You weren't a rebound or anything like that. I don't

even want to say you were a one-night stand because that's not why I went to the gym."

"Why did you go?" I ask only because I need to know even if this is the last place I wanted to have this conversation.

"I felt something the first day we met, and I know it's stupid, but I just had to know. I just went about it the wrong way."

I nod, and set my hands on her hips. "And do you?"

Before she can answer, a young punk skates by us, clipping me on the shoulder. My feet start to slip out, and all I can see is the roof as I start to fall. Yvie comes with me because in my moment of gracefulness, I forget to let her go.

We land with a thump, and the cold instantly chills me. Yvie laughs, and I quickly follow suit.

"Sorry, I should've let you go."

"I'm not," she replies, as she brushes her lips against mine. I don't let her pull away as I set my hand on the back of her head and hold her to my mouth. We shouldn't be doing this, but I don't want to stop. When her tongue tangles with mine, and her fingers push into my hair, I'm done for. She's worth getting to know, even if it means it's over in a week.

CHAPTER 9
YVIE

BABY giggles are the best. This I've just learned after listening to Eden laugh. All the kids are so well behaved with her, making her laugh and feel like she's a big girl, even though she's just over a year old. She chases them from the living room and into the dining room and the back again, and she's laughing the entire time. Each time they come back into the living room, Eden falls into Jimmy's arms. He holds her for a moment before he encourages her to get them. Then it starts all over again.

I find myself watching and waiting for their return, laughing with them. Eden is adorable with her dark, curly hair and chubby cheeks. She loves everyone, but the minute she sees her mom or dad in the room, her eyes light up.

Jenna comes into the living room with a squealing Eden in her arms. She sets her down, only for Eden to waddle-run back to wherever the other kids are.

"She's gorgeous, Jenna."

"Thanks! She's a handful, that's for sure. She's all Jimmy and has him completely wrapped around her finger."

"Quinn was the same way with Harrison. It's not hard when they're so innocent, and you can't help but fall in love with them."

This time it's Jimmy that walks in with Eden in his arms. She's patting his cheeks and saying "Daddy". I've known Jimmy for a long time, and it's hard to think that he almost wasn't here to see his daughter come into the world. The guys have always dealt with overzealous fans, but only in the form of women. I've witnessed far too many women throwing themselves at the guys, but never have they had a problem with a man until Jenna's ex wanted her back.

Jenna takes a squirming Eden from Jimmy's hands, and she tries to push Jimmy away from Jenna when he goes to kiss her. It's cute how possessive she is.

"When are you going to get up the duff?"

The slap and "ouch" that quickly follows comes as a result of Jenna slapping Jimmy. "What, Sweet Lips? It's a valid question."

"It's rude, Jimmy. Not everyone wants kids, ya know. You didn't."

"Yeah, but that was before I knocked you up good and proper." Jimmy moves out of the way before Jenna can slap him again. As soon as he's out of the room, Eden wants down.

"I don't know how you put up with Jimmy for so long," Jenna says with a shake of her head.

I shrug. "It's one of those things you just learn to deal with. He's always been like a brother to me. He's not the same though. You make him different," I say, much to her joy. Her smile is wide, and she ducks her head as she looks away.

"He's changed *me*. He put up with so much after he was shot, and then after my ex tried to... well, let's just say Jimmy has had more than enough reasons to leave me."

"I think you underestimate his love for you, Jenna. I was there when he was with Chelsea. He never looked at her the way he looks at you. You're his match."

We're interrupted by Liam, Josie and Noah opening the door and walking in, greeting us with a boisterous "Merry Christmas". It's silly that we're all here tonight at Harrison's since we'll be at Liam's tomorrow, but who am I to complain about a party with adult beverages and food? And maybe a sighting of a man who made me feel so incredibly special yesterday. When we went back to his house last night, I wanted to take things to the next level, but he was hesitant. I could see that. I don't blame him, really. I'm only visiting for a few days and probably won't see him for another year.

Jenna and I make our way into the dining room where Liam scoops me up and spins me around.

"You have to meet my wife," he says as he puts me down.

"Josie, this is Yvie, Harrison's sister, and this is my son, Noah." Hearing Liam introduce his family with so much pride in his voice reminds me that there's a different side to him. I'm used to the cynical side of Liam, and haven't seen this loving family man since Quinn was a baby. Noah waves, and quickly leaves us to chat.

"It's very nice to meet you. I've heard so much about you," Josie tells me. I wish I could say the same, but Liam never spoke about her.

"Congratulations," I say, knowing their anniversary is

coming in a few days, with yet another party to be had. I'll miss that one though, as I'm going back to New York Christmas night. As much as I'd like to stay, I have to return to work.

"Thank you. It's been an amazing two years." Josie beams at Liam who leans in for a kiss. That's my cue to make myself scarce. I glance at the door, hoping that it'll open and Xander will walk through, but no such luck. I told him yesterday how much I hated being the fifth wheel and I thought he understood.

I walk down the hall toward the kitchen and stop in the doorway, spying on Harrison and Katelyn. He has her caged against the counter, and it looks like he's telling her a secret. The look of adoration in her eyes -- that is what I want. I want to look at the man I love and know I'll never stop loving him, no matter what. My brother's life – what he's turned it into – is really something to marvel at. He's taken on the role of dad flawlessly, and done so without reservation. Not too many men, or women for that matter, would do that. I know that Quinn loves Katelyn without question.

"Hey, Mom, can we go downstairs and watch a movie?" Quinn walks in from the other side of the kitchen, and I step back so he doesn't see me.

Harrison moves away from Katelyn to give his son her undivided attention. She runs her fingers over his shaggy hair, pushing it behind his ear. "Grandma will be here soon. Xander went to pick her up from the airport and they were stopping to get Grandpa, so chose a movie that you guys won't mind shutting off for a while, okay?" Quinn nods and runs off.

So that's where Xander is. I want to be mad at him for keeping me waiting, but the fact that he's picking up my mom gives him massive bonus points. Yesterday, being with him, shopping and then ice-skating was probably one of the best days I've had in a long time. Being with Xander takes no effort at all. Everything seems to flow as if we're in sync. When I'm with Oliver, I'm always on edge. I'm constantly watching where I'm stepping, what I'm saying. My clothes have to be perfect. My hair has to be styled. I always have to be en pointe. With Oliver I feel stressed out, but he's comfortable. With Xander, I'm anxious and waiting for the other shoe to drop, so to speak.

Even the way Xander touches me is different, better. He hesitates, as if he's asking my body for permission to be caressed by him. The rise in my body temperature and the pebbling of my skin is all because of him. Yesterday, I felt seduced even though our night ended with a simple but lingering goodnight kiss. It was like he was showing me what I'm missing by not living here, or what it'd be like if he and I were together.

Even now, thinking about being with him makes my body tingle with anticipation. I'm not expecting that we'll be together like that again, or that he even wants to see me outside of our lives with my family, but I'm hoping.

The door opens, and I turn. My steps down the hall are slow as people file in. First is an older man I'm assuming is Katelyn's father-in-law, and next is my mother. She doesn't see me and that's okay because watching her interact with Mr. Powell is worth me being forgotten. He helps her with her coat, and the smile she has for him is unwavering. I'm going to have to ask Harrison what that's all about. It would be nice to see her happy with someone, anyone for that matter, as long as he treats her like a queen. She deserves it. All my life, Harrison and I were put in front of her happiness. It's time she started living for her.

As soon as my mom sees me, I'm in her arms. I've missed her so much. "Baby girl, I'm so happy you're here."

"Me too, Mom."

She pulls away and places her hands on my cheeks. There are tears in her eyes. "I'm so happy that I have my family home for Christmas."

I nod and before I can say anything, Quinn is wrapped around her waist. I'm soon forgotten, but that's okay because the man that I want to give my attention to just motioned for me to follow him into the living room.

Everything moves in slow motion for me as I walk to Xander. He's smiling, but his lower lip is pulled into his mouth. The way he's looking at me makes me wish we were alone. I don't know about him, but I'm undressing him with my eyes and know I'm not doing him justice. I need to stop thinking about him like that and just enjoy our friendship.

He kisses me on the cheek before stepping back and putting the customary space between us. "Sorry I'm late. I should've called."

"Yes, you should have," I joke, reminding myself that we're not a couple, and he doesn't owe me anything.

"I would've, but I don't have your number."

I laugh and step a little closer. My hands ache to clutch the sides of his sweater, to pull him close and whisper my number against his lips. "I could probably give you my number."

"Yeah, I'd like that," he says, leaning closer.

"What's wrong, mate? Does she have bad breath?"

We step away quickly, and both of us blush. I hear Jenna yell Jimmy's name, but the damage is done. Liam and Harrison are both standing next to him. Liam is expressionless and Harrison's eyebrow is raised. He doesn't look pissed — not that I'd care. I'm an adult and can do what I want.

Harrison runs his hand over his beanie and clears his throat. For someone who told Xander that he'd be okay with us, he's sure having a hard time finding something to say. "Uh… yeah." He looks at Liam who shrugs but doesn't bother looking at Jimmy because let's face it, anything Jimmy says will be crude. "Katelyn says the food is ready." Harrison walks away, followed by Jimmy who is laughing.

Liam takes a step into the room, his hands shoved deep into this pockets. "Don't hurt her," he says, his voice monotone.

"I won't," Xander replies quickly. He's right, he won't. There's nothing to hurt. We aren't declaring love for each other; we're just enjoying each other's company.

"We're just friends," I reply, only to realize how shitty that sounds. Xander is looking at Liam, but that does nothing to hide the fact that I've hurt him. His eyes close and Liam smirks.

As soon as Liam leaves the room, Xanders turns to face me. He's hurt. I can see it in his eyes.

"I'm sorry that was rude of me."

"It's fine," he says. "We are friends, right?"

I nod, but suddenly hate that word. None of my "friends" treat me the way Xander does. We need a better word for what we are, or what we could be.

"Do you think you can get away tonight?" he asks, much to my surprise. I could've been friend-zoned after my comment.

"I'll be there."

CHAPTER 10
XANDER

THIS is my second Christmas with the guys and their families. The first one was awkward because I felt like an outsider intruding on what little private time they actually have. This year it feels like family though and tomorrow when I arrive at Liam's, I'll be bearing presents for the kids. I actually had fun shopping for them. They're easy to buy for. The only gift I can give the guys is free membership to the gym, and they refuse to accept that. Honest friendship is all they require, and that's something I can definitely give them. Besides, what do you buy people who have everything? Nothing. That's what.

When Katelyn called and asked me to pick up Mrs. James and Mr. Powell, I had to bite my tongue to keep from telling her no. There was a certain someone that I couldn't wait to see, and by arriving late I was prolonging what my body was craving. Yvie, in the flesh.

Last night, watching her drive away from my house sent an ache right through my core. I'm falling for her hard, and I need to find a way to curb what I'm feeling. Except, I can't. Yvie James is a force to be reckoned with and bit by bit, she's inching her way into my life. I thought I could put the night in the gym behind me, but I can't. Having her in my house was killing me. I knew if I made a move, our clothes would've been pushed aside until I could be in her again. The problem is that my heart is guiding me and not my head.

The thought of asking her to stay in Beaumont has crossed my mind. Her brother and nephew are here. Her mom is here a lot, and she has a sister-in-law and two nieces to get to know. But that's not enough for someone like Yvie. The way she speaks about her goals and dreams – Beaumont can't compete with that. Hell, I can't compete with that, not that I'd even try.

I told myself this morning that my heart is shut off. This thing between Yvie and myself is nothing but a vacation hook-up. She goes back to New York tomorrow night, and I'll go back to doing what I do best, or find a new hobby. I may even start dating. There are plenty of eligible women here… once I find one who wants me for me and not for my connection to the band.

So why I can't I stay away? Why can't I walk into a room and not make eye contact with her? Until I met Yvie, I thought I had to have what everyone else described: the electricity, the fire that burns when you touch the person you're meant to be with. No one said anything about the magnetic pull that someone can have on you. *That* is what I'm feeling. Yvie is the energy source feeding my addiction.

It was never my intention for us to get caught in a compromising situation, and I should've known better than to pull her aside in a house full of people, especially her family, but I couldn't resist. I had to be near her to see if she's feeling the same way I am.

"We should join them," I tell her, nodding toward the other room. Yvie smiles and starts to walk way, solidifying my thought that we're working toward two different goals. Mine needs to be protecting my heart. I don't know what hers is, and honestly I'm not willing to find out. If I'm lucky enough to have her again, it's going to be nothing but sex.

I don't realize how long I stay in the other room watching her walk out of my life until I enter the dining room. Christmas music is playing and eggnog is flowing.

"Tonight, the night before our kids become more spoiled, is for letting loose and enjoying our family. As parents, we know how stressful and exciting tomorrow is, so we all need a little relaxation," Liam says, raising his glass. I quickly grab one and follow suit. "Tonight, let's be adults while our children are making their last minute wish lists."

"Here, here," everyone says as our glasses clank together.

Yvie is across the room next to her mom and Katelyn, and she's focused on them. This is how it should be. We aren't a couple and my betraying heart implied that we were when I arrived earlier. I can't make that mistake again.

"So you and Yvie?"

Jimmy pats me on the shoulder, as if to congratulate me. Only he doesn't know that there's nothing to celebrate.

"Nah," I say with a shake of my head. "We're just friends."

"That's too bad, mate. She needs a good bloke like you around. That arse she's been with is a total loser."

"So I hear." I haven't really because we haven't talked about him much. I honestly don't care about him and if he succeeds in getting her back, he's one lucky bastard in my book. But if I find out he tells her she has a fat ass, I may just have to fly to New York and beat his.

I hate that these thoughts are running through my head. I need to be enjoying the moment and not thinking about what it's going to be like when she goes. She's leaving, there's no question about that. Yvie's been pretty damn clear from the get-go she's only here visiting.

"You'd treat her better."

There's no doubt about that, but it's never going to happen. "Are you telling me that I should move to New York?"

"What the bloody hell are you going on about? Yvie needs to move here, and you're the one that could make it happen."

My gaze falls onto Yvie, who happens to look in my direction. Her smile is infectious, and I find myself returning one.

"JD, even I don't have the power to make a woman change her mind. Yvie has a career in New York, a life. Beaumont doesn't have anything to offer her."

"That's where you're wrong. Take a look around you. We're her family. If she knows you can give her all this as well as a happy life, what more could she want?"

I down the rest of my eggnog and turn toward him. "Women like Yvie are just like you. You crave the bright lights, the fans and the stardom that comes with doing something you love. Unlike you though, where you can set up a studio anywhere, she can't. Broadway holds all her dreams so unless I gave up my business and followed her, I'm strictly in the friend zone."

I have to walk away from Jimmy for two reasons: one,

he makes everything seem so simple and two, because he's right. She does belong here, but she'll never be here as long as her dream is there. Sadly, there isn't anything we can do about our dreams.

EADLIGHTS shine into my window, illuminating my dark living room. I bailed on Harrison's the first chance I could get. After my conversation with JD, I just couldn't be there anymore. I never thought I would fall so fast for someone, but I have. When I think about my future, I see Yvie standing next to me. I know it's all a part of my imagination, and I just need to get over it. Everything will be fine once she goes back home. I'll be able to move on with my life, and she'll fulfill her dreams. It's a win-win for the both of us.

I'm opening the door before she finishes knocking. Yvie steps in, and I slide my arm around her waist, pulling her to me with a little force. She smiles, biting her lower lip, teasing me. I shut the door and push her coat off her shoulders, letting it fall to the floor. I should stop now, but I can't. I want this with her even if my heart breaks in the morning.

"You left me," she whispers in the darkness. My fingers trail along her cheekbone.

"I didn't think you'd notice." I place a tiny kiss on each side of her mouth.

"How could I not?" she whispers, as my teeth tug on her earlobe. Her hands slide under my shirt and move until she's tracing my pecs with her fingernails. I step back and pull my shirt over my head because I like the way she's exploring my chest and don't want her hands restricted.

"I see you were expecting me?" she says, pulling on

my already loose belt.

"I was getting comfortable." I crouch down and run my hands over her legs. She's wearing a red sweater dress with black boots that go to her knees. All night I thought about what lies beneath. I trail my hands up her legs, pushing up her dress as I go. I stand and pull her dress over her head.

"Oh fuck," I blurt out when I'm rewarded with her perfect breasts covered in black lace. I suck one into my mouth and her nails dig into my back. My heart is yelling at me to stop while both my brains are telling me to go faster.

I pick her up and her legs squeeze around my hips as I carry her up to my room. Each step I take is done so blindly since my lips haven't left her breasts. I pay equal attention to both until we reach my room.

Setting her down on my bed gently, I slip off her boots and she slides down her tights. Her beautiful porcelain skin looks alabaster against my dark comforter with the moonlight shining through.

"You're so beautiful," I say against her skin. I shed my pants before I crawl up next to her. We're side by side and we're at the point of no return. We could stop and pretend the other night didn't happen, or we could cross into the friends-with-benefits zone. Even though I'm not getting everything I want, I'm still with her. Fuck it!

My hand trails down her side, her skin pebbling from my touch. She hitches her leg over my hip, telling me what she wants. I'm not one to deny her, and I slip my finger into her panties. Her eyes start to close, but she fights it. She's watching me watch her as my finger works her over. Her heel pushes into my ass, encouraging me. When her hips start to rock, I know she's close. I'm a selfish man and want to feel her clench around my cock and not my finger.

I sit up and rip her panties away from her and unclasp her bra. She follows and pushes my boxers off of me, taking me in her hand. My eyes roll back, and I can't help but thrust into her hand.

"Do you want me?" she asks, as she lies back down. I inch forward and rub the head of my cock against her clit.

"Is this what you want?"

She bites her lip and nods. I push in slowly and hiss at the connection. I keep going, pulling out and starting over. My hands cup her breast as I slide in and out of her. Her head falls back, her eyes closing. I lean forward and capture her mouth, pressing my body against hers. We move in unison, creating friction and heat.

"You're so beautiful." I kiss her again, increasing my tempo. She moans, her nails pressing into my back.

"Fuck, you're so wet, Yvie." Her hands trail down my back and push into my ass, and I move faster. She screams out, asking for more. I flip her over, not giving her time to adjust before I'm slipping into her again. I pull her up, using her flexibility to my advantage. I hold her to my chest, my hand fondling her breast. She rocks into me as my finger finds her clit. I rub her frantically, feeling that she's close.

"Alexander," she let's my name fall from her lips in ecstasy. I increase my ministrations, pushing into her with all that I am.

"Fuck," I groan when I feel her squeeze my cock. Yvie pants as I reach my climax. We fall forward, in a heap of sweat and heavy breathing.

I roll over, pulling out of her, but taking her with me. "That was…"

"Orgasmic," she says, with a laugh.

I chuckle and kiss the top of her head before getting up and heading toward the bathroom. I clean up, and bring back a wet washcloth for her.

Crawling toward her, I let the cloth lead a path up her body. She shivers, but doesn't push me away. Yvie takes the washcloth from me and throws it over my face. I pull it down in time to watch her walk out of room, naked.

I close my eyes, and wait for her to return. I want to keep her and not let her go back to New York, but that's not possible. When she comes back, she crawls over my body, stopping to blow on my semi-hard dick. He starts to spring to life again as she lays her body over mine. I hold her there, relishing in the moment.

"You called me Alexander; I think that made me come."

Yvie laughs. "I found your name on a piece of paper at my brother's. I was going to call you Alexander earlier, but it just slipped out there."

"I like the way it sounds coming off your lips." I instantly regret saying those words, and we both go quiet. "Hey, can I take you to the airport tomorrow?"

"I have a rental car," she says, sitting up partially so I can see her.

"Harrison and I can take care of it. I'd just feel better if you let me drive you."

She nods. "Okay, Alexander."

I growl and roll over the top of her. "Say it again, and you'll be sorry." I thrust my hips into hers, showing her that I'm ready and willing for another round.

"Show me what you have, Alexander Knight." I push into her and that shuts her up. As I move over the top of her, I realize that this woman, whether she's a friend or lover, is going to be the death of me.

CHAPTER 11
YVIE

I'S four in the morning when I open the door to Harrison's house. The walk of shame has never felt as good as it does now, but with that I'm fighting back the tears and heartbreak for a friend. It was evident tonight that Xander may want more than what I can offer. I'm not a mind reader, but body language speaks volumes and his was yelling.

I should listen, but in doing so I would be admitting that I'm ready to give up on my dream. Falling into a pattern, an easy life, with Xander would be so easy and refreshing if he just lived in New York. That's where I've wanted to be ever since I was a little girl. I dreamt of dancing on the big stage in front the biggest crowds, and I'm almost there. Even with *Enchantment* being on Broadway, my theater is small. I strive for the grander theaters with the crystal chandeliers so big you imagine yourself swinging from them. Dancing is a childhood dream that I've never given up on.

I turn on the Christmas tree and watch the white lights twinkle against the ornaments. Sitting down on the couch, I wrap up in the afghan and marvel at the presents under the tree. Five people live in this house and there are enough gifts under there that I feel overwhelmed. This will be my biggest Christmas ever, and I'm just here to watch.

"Just getting home?"

I startle at the sound of Harrison's voice. He saunters into the living room and takes the seat next to me, stealing some of the afghan.

"Can't sleep, Santa?"

He looks at me and shrugs. "What's going on with you? We haven't really spent a lot of time together since you arrived."

"You're busy, and I sort of just showed up on your doorstep. I didn't expect you to drop everything and entertain me. I'm a big girl. I can fend for myself."

"I'm still your brother. I'll always make time for you. You know that."

I nod, knowing that he'll do whatever he can to make me happy. I stare at the tree, letting the colors from the ornaments and lights blend in. "Remember when we were little and we'd try to stay awake to see Santa? We'd get so excited when we woke up and there were some presents under the tree only to get to school and hear about all the toys that everyone got. I used to lie to my friends and tell them that I got that Barbie everyone else did and you pulled her head off. When I got older it was clothes. I'd lie and whine to my friends that "the hottest jeans ever" shrunk when I washed them. I felt so bad but couldn't tell people the truth.

"Look at what you've done for Quinn and even the

twins." I nod toward the tree. "It looks like a toy store exploded under here and in a few hours they'll come thundering down the stairs to tear open everything under that tree. Within ten minutes it'll be over."

"We open our stockings first, eat breakfast and then I sit down and hand out a present at time. Katelyn and I like to see their expressions for each gift. It makes it last longer." Harrison sighs. "You know when I first got here, Peyton was being bullied at school and Quinn sucker punched the kid. I was angry at him, but also thrilled that he did that for her. I wish someone had done that for me because then maybe I wouldn't hate my childhood so much. There wasn't anything Mom could do about it either so I never told her. Had I not found those drums, we'd probably still be living in that dump of an apartment."

Harrison pats my leg and stares off. I don't want to think about what our lives would be like if he hadn't come across the discarded drums in that alley way. I wouldn't be where I am today. Once he started playing, he did anything he could to make money. First it was five dollars then ten. That ten became a hundred quickly. The first time he was paid a hundred for a gig, he took Mom and me out to dinner. It wasn't anything fancy, but to us it was like we were eating at the Ritz.

He gave up college for me and always made sure I had money for dance lessons. When the private dance company offered me a spot, he took a day job and started living off two to three hours of sleep a night to provide for us. As soon as the gig opened at *Metro* he was able to cut back, and then everything changed when Liam got signed and took Harrison with him. Liam made Harrison feel like he mattered.

"What's going on with you, Yvie? You dodged the question. I'm not trying to pry, but you don't seem yourself."

I poke my fingers through the holes on the afghan to avoid looking at Harrison. He pulls my hand away. He's not going to let this go. I thought that I could show up and everyone would just be happy. We'd do family activities, and I'd be on my way back before anyone could figure out what's going on with me.

"Have you ever felt that you weren't good enough?"

Harrison groans. He relaxes into the couch, putting his hands behind his head. "Every day. I'm always questioning whether I'm a good enough father, a good enough partner for Katelyn. Can I be better? What can I do to improve? I'm no different than you, Yvie. I remember what we came from and how we got here."

"How *you* got us here, Harrison. Don't short change yourself."

He shakes his head. "We did this. If I didn't have the support from you and Mom, I would've never gone out and started playing in public. Everything that has happened to us did so for a reason. We struggled, but we overcame it and now I want to know why you think you're not good enough."

"He tells me I'm not. He tells me I'm fat, or that I don't extend properly. He tells me my hair isn't pulled tight enough."

"Oliver?" he asks and I nod, wiping away a tear. "Is that why you left him?"

"Yes, and he wants to settle down and I don't, at least not with him, but I'm so torn because he can make or break my career. I want to leave *Enchantment*, but am afraid he'll give me a bad reputation, and I can't afford that."

Harrison pulls me into his arms, and I let the tears fall. It's Christmas, and I shouldn't be crying — especially over Oliver.

"What's up with you and Xander?"

I pull back and wipe at my cheeks. "I like him, but he's here and I'm there. We're friends and it's good to have friends, especially someone who isn't in the business."

"Yeah, I know what that's like."

Harrison trails off and the room grows quiet. It's only a matter of time before the kids wake up and the house is crazy.

"Have you ever talked to Liam about how he ended up in California?"

I shake my head.

"Do me a favor and ask him today when we go over. His story might help you figure out yours." He leans over and gives me a kiss on the cheek before getting up and leaving the room. He starts banging around in the kitchen, making enough noise to wake the house.

The first one down is my mom, and when Harrison returns with coffee, the three of us cuddle on the couch. We haven't done this in years, and it feels good. Five minutes later, Katelyn comes down, followed shortly by Quinn. He climbs in between my mom and me, and Katelyn takes an awkward family Christmas photo. It's going to be one that I look at every day to remember this morning. As soon as the girls wake, the stockings are passed around. When Katelyn hands me one with my name on it, I can't fight the tears. It's easy to see how Harrison fell for her so fast.

Once breakfast is done, Harrison dons a Santa hat and starts the process of handing out present by present. Each time my name is called, my heart stops a little. By the time we're done, we have just enough time to shower and head over to Liam and Josie's. The thought of seeing Xander has me on edge. Memories of last night haven't escaped my mind all morning. Each time I'm not focusing on what's going on around me, it's because I'm reliving last night.

The night we had in the gym was erotic and I'll never forget it, but standing there in his room with the moonlight shining through the window as his fingers moved lightly over my skin, is engrained in my mind forever. The softness of his lips as they created a fiery path over my body is still being felt. The way my fingers curled around his hard muscles when he rocked into me. Knowing that he was the cause of my head falling back and my eyes closing on their own free will is something I've never experienced before. We were slow and precise, everything that we weren't before. There wasn't a piece of flesh that our mouths didn't cover. He was making love and that scares the shit out of me.

THE kids run into the house, yelling and screaming as Josie and Liam greet us at the door. Kisses and hugs are exchanged as if we haven't seen each other for years, not hours. Liam and Josie's house is almost twice the size of Harrison and Katelyn's and decorated like a window display on Fifth Avenue. Garland, lights, and red ribbons are everywhere, reminding me of home.

"Would you like a tour?" Liam asks when he catches me looking around. I smile sheepishly as he takes my hand and starts showing me around. We start upstairs and he shows me Noah's room and the room where all the magic happens. I pretend to gag and slip out of his grasp when he rubs his knuckles on my hair.

We walk down the stairs to the basement and when he flips the light on, the studio comes to life.

"*This* is the magic room," I say, staring into their

recording room.

"Yeah, I guess. We're getting ready to go on tour again. It's big this time though. The kids won't be able to join us until schools out."

"No tutor?"

Liam shakes his head. "Noah plays baseball, and I don't want him to miss it."

"What about you missing his games?"

Liam pulls out a chair and sits down. "I'm torn, but this is my job. I'm not the only musician with kids, and they all make it work. I think it's because I haven't always been there that it's more of a problem."

"That's not your fault."

Liam's crinkles his face. "I know, but it still hurts them when I leave."

I lean against the wall and realize that Liam is probably a little bit like me. When I first met him I had a crush on him, but Harrison nipped that quickly. It didn't take long before I saw Liam as a brother and not a love interest.

"Can I ask you something?"

"Sure, what's up?" he leans on the desk, clasping his hands.

"Why did you leave?" I bite the inside of my cheek, afraid of what his reaction is going to be.

Liam rubs his hands over his face and sighs. "Everyone had this idea of what I was going to be and when I went to college, I realized that wasn't who I was. I was too afraid to tell the people that I loved the most that I was unhappy. I was heading for the biggest drug-induced downward spiral without the drugs and just left everyone and everything behind."

"Do you have any regrets?"

He shakes his head. "I don't. Had I stayed, Josie and I probably wouldn't be married. I'd likely be an accountant or a teacher, living in a run-down house and seeing my kid on the weekends. Things happened for a reason, and while yes, I missed ten years, I had to in order to find myself. I probably sound selfish and I don't mean to be, but you can't live your life by someone else's dreams. They have to be your own and just because it was a dream at one point, doesn't mean it's your dream now. The beautiful thing about dreams is that they're ever changing."

The lights flicker, causing Liam to laugh. "It's time for dinner, or linner – that's what Noah calls it because we're eating dinner at lunch time."

Liam puts his arm around me and we walk up the stairs, bumping our shoulders into each other with each step we take. When we open the door, everyone is gathered around the table, including Xander. When he sees me, his smile is wide, but he keeps his head down. I know what he's thinking about — his red cheeks give him away. It's okay, though, because I've been thinking about it all day, too.

Once dinner is done, the kids open more presents. Watching Eden open hers is funny. She gets so excited for the box but doesn't care about what's inside. As I look around, I see my brother with his girlfriend, wife, his life partner and can see how happy they are. My other brothers, Liam and Jimmy, both married and with kids, are happy. Their smiles are genuine and not forced. I don't know if this is something I can have or not, but I don't see Oliver fitting in with my family, and this is what he wants. He wants a big family, holidays and birthday parties. I want it too, but I also want to be center stage.

Xander hands me an eggnog and tells me it's adult flavored. This will calm my nerves for my flight later. I hate that I have rehearsals tomorrow and have a feeling Oliver did that so that I'd have to come right back. Sometimes I think he does things to be malicious so I can cry on his shoulder. I'm done with that though. I need to be able to stand on my own two feet.

The night beckons and all too soon, it's time for me to leave. Xander offered to drive me to the airport so I say my goodbyes at Liam's. I hug everyone and am surprised that Peyton is waiting for one.

"Thanks for my necklace," she says as I pull away. I see the delicate silver chain hanging from her neck and my pride swells. I need to get to know these girls and be an aunt to them.

"I'll see you guys soon," I say, as I walk out the door and rush to Xander's car. He's already transferred my suitcase from Harrison's to his. He and Harrison will return my rental for me tomorrow. I balked at first when Xander offered to take me, but the thought of having him for the ride to the airport would be worth it.

We hold hands throughout the drive, but don't speak. The air between us is heavy and I know we should talk about what happened last night, but I'm not sure what to say. I don't want to cheapen what we did by adding unnecessary words.

Xander guides me into the airport after parking his car. He waits while I check in and walks me to security. I fall into his arms, and let him hold me. I'm going to miss him more than I can find the words to tell him.

When I look up at him, he cups my face and kisses me softly. His lips linger on mine for a moment before I make a move to deepen the kiss. I know I'm leading him on, but I'm leading myself on too. I need this last memory of him on my lips before I board that plane.

"You have my number, right?"

I laugh. Earlier this morning, he put his number in my phone and texted himself, marveling at how excellent he is in bed. I saved that text message.

"I do. I'm sure I'll be using it."

"Remember: no sexting while I'm working." He laughs and kisses me one more time.

"I can't make any promises," I say, winking. He blushes and shakes his head.

One last kiss and I'm making my way through security. I wave at him before I turn the corner and disappear down the hall. My phone chimes, and I roll my eyes. He can't even wait until I was home before he texts. I pull out my phone and tap my message icon.

> **Lindsey: Thought you should know Oliver has been spending time with Cami, and she's on the list as the lead for tomorrow.**

I stop dead in my tracks. Cami is my rival and much younger than I am. Let's face it, I'm no spring chicken, but I take care of myself and I work hard to retain my youthful appearance. She has been after my role for months. I've caught her a few times flirting with Oliver, but he assured me he wasn't interested in her. If she's taking my spot that only means one thing. They're sleeping together. I know I have no room to talk, but I've never been with him to advance my career. If she's taking the lead, I don't have practice for a few days. I look around at the lack of people traveling today and wonder what I'm doing.

I look down at my phone and pull up Xander's message from earlier. The message from him gloating about his prowess stares back at me. I don't know what I'm doing, or what I want, but maybe if I spend more time with him and my family I can figure it out.

Do you have plans for New Years Eve?

CHAPTER 12
XANDER

MY car is cold even though the heater is on and blowing warm air. I feel the loss of Yvie already, and it's only been a few minutes. I told myself that getting involved with her emotionally would be a mistake, and everything in my head is telling me that it is – *was* – but my heart is telling me to hang on and to keep her in my life in any capacity that she'll allow.

Yesterday, last night, whatever you want to call it, wasn't supposed to happen. After talking to JD and realizing that Yvie and I are on two different paths in life, I knew I had to shut down. But when she pulled up, I had my front door open before she could even knock. My mind was made up; I was going to take everything that she was willing to give and not let go, until now.

Leaving her in the airport, watching her disappear out of sight is the worst feeling I've ever experienced. The rock I seem to have swallowed is pushing against my heart, lungs and stomach. I can't get comfortable whether I sit up, stand or clear my throat to dislodge the solid mass that has taken residency there. The pressure increases with each movement.

The warm air becomes stifling and my chest aches, a feeling that I despise. I've kept myself free from entanglements, only dating here and there and never anything too serious. I've waited for that one special person to walk into my life, and now that she has, she's walked right back out. I don't think I knew she was the one until this moment and now that I know, I'm not sure what I can do to show her how I feel. She needs to know that us being together while she was here wasn't just about sex for me. Thing is, it may have been that way for her. If so, I can handle it. She doesn't need to know how I feel. Guys are best at compartmentalizing their feelings anyway.

I roll down my window and take a gulp of air. I don't know why I'm stalling. I don't know why I'm still parked and not driving back home or to the gym. It's not like she's going to come running out and fall into my arms. She's heading back to New York where she lives and works. I have to accept that. I have to find a way to be her friend and stay present in her life. I refuse to go away unless she asks me to. If I have to resort to making her smile via video chat, then so be it. I'll be the best damn video chatter ever.

Slipping my car into reverse, I pull out of the parking spot and into drive. I tell myself that seeing her via a computer is better than nothing, and I'm not going to wait for her to call me. I'm going to take the initiative so she knows I'm interested. My phone beeps, and I glance at the screen. I stop in the middle of the lane and stare at Yvie's name on my screen. My fingers twitch as I slide my thumb over her name and her message appears.

> *Tiny Dancer: Do you have plans for New Year's Eve?*

I put my car in park and read her text message again. My automatic response is to say 'you', but we won't be together so I tell her exactly what I hope to be doing.

> *I'd love to spend it with you, but since we won't be together seeing you through my phone or computer will have to do.*

I hit send before I can erase the cheese oozing out of my message. I really need to be more manly and less of a sissy. I set down my phone and try to resist checking it constantly to see if she'll text back right away. I could park and just text her until she has to turn off her phone, or I can leave.

My decision is made for me when my phone beeps, and her name shows on my screen again

> *Tiny Dancer: I'm not going back until after NYE. Can you come get me???*

My eyes bug out of my head when I read her message. I read it again just to make sure I comprehend everything clearly. I throw my car into reverse and drive as fast as I can back to the spot I just vacated. Backing in, my door is open before I even put my car in park. My heart is racing with anticipation and dread. What if she's only asking me to get her because I just dropped her off? Realistically, I'm the closest and her brother is still celebrating Christmas and has probably had a few too many to drink. Katelyn could come get her, but maybe Yvie wants me to pick her up.

I speed walk back toward the terminal, trying not to look eager. I didn't respond to her message, and I don't want her to think I'm ignoring her. Yvie stands on the curb chatting with the attendant, and a pang of jealousy courses through me when he brushes something off her jacket. My walk turns to a slow here-I-come jog.

"Yvie," I yell out, not only to get her attention, but to get that of the attendant who should be checking people in curbside.

She sidesteps the man and smiles. I slow down and take in the moment. I'm going to spend New Year's Eve with the beauty that is only a few feet away from me. This may be a cause for a resolution even though I don't believe in them.

When I reach her, I cup her face and pull her to my lips. We may have only parted a half hour ago, but this guy standing here doesn't know that. And if Yvie told him by chance, then he knows I'm marking my territory, even if it's temporary.

"Are you ready?" I ask as my hands slide from her cheek and one moves over her shoulder and down her arm until my fingers are nestled in between hers. She nods, and I reach around her to grab the handle to her suitcase.

"What happened?" I'm not trying to burst my little bubble of happiness right now, but I'm curious. She's never failed to remind me that she was leaving tonight.

Yvie stops us in our tracks, her hand remaining in mine. I give her fingers a light squeeze.

"I got a text from a friend, and it wasn't the best news. It made me do a lot of thinking, and I figured I'd rather spend the rest of my year here." She shrugs as if it's no big deal that she didn't get on her flight to NYC.

"A lot of thinking in…" I look at my watch and smirk. "Thirty minutes or so?"

She steps forward, bridging the gap between us. "Sometimes all it takes is a few words for someone to realize that they're not ready to leave."

I lean forward and kiss her forehead. "Well, whatever you found out, I'm happy you decided to stay here. Let's get you home."

I start to walk, but she pulls me back. I look at her questioningly. "I was thinking I could stay with you tonight?"

She doesn't have to ask me twice. I nod quickly and pull her just a bit harder to get her moving. I've never been so excited to get home until now.

CHAPTER 13
YVIE

'M naked and warm. I'm cocooned in the arms of a man that I just met and who makes me feel beautiful and desired, who makes me feel cherished and extremely sexy. The moment I read Lindsay's text, my mind was made up to stay. I had thought about it all day yesterday. I didn't want to leave my family so quickly, and when Peyton thanked me for her necklace my heart broke at the knowledge that I couldn't spend more time with her. My opportunity to get to know her better was flashing like a beacon and there wasn't anything I could do about it.

I never thought Oliver would do that – replace me with my understudy – because I took some personal time during our hiatus. This is his way of showing me who's the boss, and I'm fine with that. I can go back to work with my head held high and throw the biggest diva bullshit move he's ever seen. If he thinks, for one moment, that

I'm going to sit by and let some two-bit slut take away my lead, he's got another thing coming. If he has issues with my form, he must be training her hard to fix hers. There's a reason she's an understudy. Unless, of course, the only form he's concerned with is the one she's mastering while on her knees.

"You're hurting my hand and thinking far too hard for this early in the morning," Xander mumbles into this crook of my neck. I've never been a cuddler, but being in his arms like this makes me never want to leave. He has a king-size bed, and we're smack dab in the middle. No his side, no her side. Not that I have a side, but being in his arms makes me feel like I could.

I hadn't realized I was squeezing his hand until he said something. I ease up on my grip and try to move closer to him. There's little space, if any, and my movements cause him to groan. I stifle a laugh and don't say anything. With my back against his chest, I wiggle again and his hand clamps down on my hip.

"You're going to be the death of me." He nuzzles deeper into my neck and places his lips against my shoulder.

"Oh, well we can't have that." I start to pull away, only to be pulled back against this chest as he continues peppering my neck and shoulder with kisses. His scruff brushes against my skin, causing goosebumps. My hand reaches down in between us, finding him ready and hopefully willing. It never occurred to me what it would mean to Xander when I texted him last night asking him to come back and get me. I want to ask him where he sees us going, but the truth of the matter is, I can't see past next week. I'd be foolish to make any type of gesture with him that might lead him on. Besides, long-distance relationships don't work out, and our schedules really aren't conducive to even trying.

Xander pulls my hand, leaving me with me no choice but to let go of him. He moves us slightly, locking our conjoined hands down onto the bed and pushes my leg up with his, giving him the perfect angle to take me. His cock brushes against me, and I hiss. I'm sensitive after last night and early this morning. Xander has a healthy appetite for sex, not that I'm complaining.

He pulls back and sits up on his elbow. "Are you sore?" he asks as he takes his hand away from mine and trails his fingers over my exposed breast. My skin pebbles, and my nipples peak. Xander doesn't wait for an answer as he licks my nipple, pulling the bud with his teeth. His hips thrust as he rubs his hard on along my pussy.

"Answer me, Yvie. If you're sore, I'll stop."

"Don't stop," I beg as Xander eases into me slowly. I'm sore, but this is worth the ache. His hips move into mine as his mouth dances over my breast. This position is new for me and even though I can feel him deep, I don't like that I can't touch him freely. I slide my hand under his arm and let my nails dig into his skin. This encourages him to move faster, and he does.

Xander pushes my shoulder and buries me into his bed, his chest heavy on my back until he sits back on his knees. His hands grip my hips, pulling them back to meet his thrust.

"Oh, God," I pant out barely able to catch my breath. The sounds of heavy breathing, moaning and our skin slapping against each other turns me on. I move against him, creating more friction. His hands cup my breasts and his fingers pull on my nipples. I scream out in pleasure. With my breasts in his hand, he uses them as leverage to sit me up. My legs slide in between his and his hands guide me up and down. Xander presses his forehead to my back, allowing me to work against him.

When his finger touches my clit I'm done for. "Oh fuck," he says against my skin. "I can feel you squeezing my dick." His words and his touch are what I need to push me over the edge. I rock against him faster, more eager, forgetting that I'm sore as he rubs my clit.

"I'm…"

"I know, baby," he says as he pushes me back down onto my hands and pumps in and out of me feverishly. Xander slams into me, screaming out as his cock pulses. His hips slow, but he still moves in me, making sure I'm fully sated.

I collapse in a heap, and he quickly follows alongside me. We're both on our stomachs, looking at each other. I want to ask him what he's thinking, but now is not the time. He's likely, just like I am, going to say something stupid and ruin the moment. I know mine would be to tell him that he's the best lover I've ever had, and I can't get the sensation of the way his muscles move under my fingertips to leave my memory. I've tried, but to no avail.

"I need to shower," he says, breaking the tension in the room. "I have to open the gym today. Care to join me?"

"At the gym?" I ask, sitting up on my elbows. The last time I was in his gym for a workout, but I got one that I wasn't expecting.

"Both," he tells me as he kisses my nose then mouth. "Come to work with me after we shower. There's a room I use for storage that has mirrors in it. We could clean it out, and you can practice."

I look at him questioningly. "Why didn't you tell me about this room before?"

Xander shrugs. "Watching you work out the other night was the hottest thing I've ever seen. No way in hell was I going to pass that up."

I move to slap him on the chest, but he grabs my wrist and pulls me into a searing kiss. He bites at my lower lip when he pulls away. "Come shower with me. Help me live out yet another fantasy."

I laugh and watch his very fine-toned ass walk away from me. I get up and shuffle down the hall. He's already in the shower with the water running when I enter the bathroom. "How many fantasies do you have?" I ask as I step in alongside him. He moves aside so that the hot water can wash over me.

"Hmm, let's see," he says as he lathers a bar of soap between his hands. I can't help but think about how smooth his hands are going to be when he touches me. "There was the gym. Ever since I bought it, I've had that fantasy but would've never done anything about it… until you came along. What we just did, having you sit up against me like that, that was definitely one." Xander's hands start roaming. The softness of the soap and the roughness of his hands creates the most divine friction against my skin. My head falls back when he kisses my pelvic bone. I think about hitching my leg over his shoulder and grabbing the shower door to hang on, but I don't want to come off as eager. He turns me around, and I miss my opportunity. "My other would be to have you in my shower, but I know you're sore so maybe next time." He bites my butt cheek and stands, ending the fun little game he was playing.

I turn around and look at him, he's hard again and stroking himself. He doesn't care that I'm watching, or that he's doing it in front of me. I bite my lip and sink down to my knees. My hands cup his ass, and my fingers dig into his skin. His hand drops and my mouth takes over where his hand left off.

"Yeah, this is definitely a fantasy."

CHAPTER 14
XANDER

STAND in the doorway and watch Yvie go through her dance routine. Today, she's looking more like a ballerina than she did the other night. Her hair is up in a bun, just like the many pictures of her at Harrison's house. She wears a black leotard, a piece of clothing that I am now very fond of. Yvie moves with such grace and poise, it's easy to see how much she loves to dance. It's also easy to see that she belongs on stage and that I should probably encourage her to not give up on her dream.

When the song ends, I start clapping. Pure joy spreads across her face. She walks, prances is more like it, and turns off her mp3 player.

"How long have you been standing there?"

"Just a few minutes," I say, stepping into the room. Yvie and I were able to move most of the stuff easily into the corner to give her enough space to dance. Once it was clean, and I pulled down the fabric cover on one of the walls, we realized that this room used to be used for dance. The wall is floor to ceiling with mirrors with existing brackets to hold a barre. I made the mistake of telling her that I'd get it cleaned up so that she had a place to practice. It didn't escape my notice that her eyes shifted, a subtle reminder that she's leaving yet again.

"Did you like what you saw?" she asks, as she twirls in the middle of the room. I walk up to her, and she stops in front of me. I take her hand and spin her around, once. Seeing her face light up from my one sorry dance move is worth being cheesy for a second.

"That's pretty good, Mr. Knight. Is there a night of dancing in our future?"

I shake my head and place my hands on her hips. I pull her close and sway even though there's no music playing. "I'm a mean slow dancer, but that's about it."

Yvie laughs and leans back, encouraging me to dip her. I do and welcome the feeling of her breasts brushing against me when I pull her up. "I could teach you how to dance," she says, turning in my arms and leaning her back to my front. Her hips start to move against mine and her arm comes up and her hand cups the back of my neck as she grinds against me.

"If this is dancing, I could get used to it." Yvie giggles and keeps us moving. I press my lips to her shoulder and continue to move along with her. I plan to take her out on a date while she's here. *Ralph's* throws a pretty big New Year's Eve party, and *4225 West* is playing. I'm sure she'll want to watch her brother perform while she's here.

As I kiss along her shoulder, all I can think about is taking her back to my house. When I get to her ear, I pull her lobe gently and whisper, "Will you be my date for Liam and Josie's anniversary party tomorrow?"

She stops moving and turns in my arms. Her hands

ghost up my arms, over my shoulders until her fingers are playing with the scruff on my face. I didn't have time to shave this morning, and right now I'm enjoying the way her fingers feel against my skin.

"You know I have my own invite."

"They don't know you're here," I remind her. "We could show up together and surprise them."

We start swaying again, and I take this opportunity to kiss her. I know I shouldn't since I'm at work, but all thoughts of professionalism are out the door the moment our tongues touch. Now all I'm thinking about is pushing her up against the mirror and watching her face as I take her from behind. She has awoken so many fantasies that I feel like a pervert trying to get them all done before she leaves. The last thing I want is for our relationship, or whatever this is, to be based solely on sex. I want to know her. I want to be her friend. I want to be her lover and confidant, even if it means that once this week is over, we're only friends. I can be her shoulder to cry on or the person she needs to vent to at the end of the night.

"Excuse me, Xander?"

I startle at the sound of my name and pull away from Yvie mid-kiss. I look over my shoulder and find Dana, the waitress from *Whimsicality*, standing in the doorway. My hands fall away from Yvie, and I turn to Dana.

"Hey, Dana, what's up?"

Dana is usually all smiles when I see her, but not today. "We have an appointment. I can reschedule if you're too busy." She leans a little to the left to get a good look at Yvie. I look at the clock on the wall and nod.

"I'll be right out. Go ahead and start on your warm-up." Dana doesn't respond, but takes a long look at me before walking away.

"She likes you," Yvie says from behind me. When I

turn around, she's back at her mp3 player, and it looks like she's scrolling through her music.

"I'm just her trainer. She works for Josie at the café." I walk toward her needing to feel her against my skin, even if it's just the palm of my hand.

Yvie doesn't make eye contact and doesn't respond to my touch. "Nonetheless, she wasn't very happy to find you in a compromising position with another woman."

I lift Yvie's chin with my thumb and forefinger and make sure she's looking at me. "It's only compromising if we're doing something wrong. We're both adults, and the last time I checked we were both very consenting." I lean forward and place a chaste kiss on her lips. "You practice. I'm going to go do what I do best," I say as I slap her ass and walk away. She lets out a little yelp, but all I do is chuckle and leave the room.

I like that Yvie is jealous; it means she cares. I can't read into her reaction though. It could be as simple as another woman interrupting her time with me. Deep down, I want it to be jealousy. I want her to question the feelings that I'm developing for her, even if she's not on the same page. She should know that I like her, more than like her actually.

HELP Yvie out of my car, appraising her short, sequined, red dress and heels that make her almost as tall as me. It's a good thing her brother is here because I have a feeling I'll be beating off guys with the tables and chairs. I feel a little underdressed compared to her. I'm only in a black button down and slacks. I started to change, but when she told me I looked hot, I didn't want to disappoint her.

We walk hand in hand into *Ralph's*, tonight's host

for Liam and Josie's anniversary party. It's by invitation only, and the guest list is long. Liam uses this as a charity event and invites industry people. Tonight, Beaumont is the place to be. One would think that Liam would have a private party, but his marriage to Josie is a reason for him to celebrate from what I've been told.

Ralph's has been transformed into a Hollywood hotspot. Strobe lights, mixed with other colored lighting create the atmosphere for tonight. On stage is the hottest DJ on the charts right now and the dance floor is full. As I look around, I realize that Yvie is used to this scene and is dressed perfectly for it. Maybe Hollywood is her next calling because I really can't see her fitting in Beaumont for an extended period of time.

Yvie pulls me onto the dance floor, even though I told her that slow dancing was my forte. I'm a white boy with no rhythm and my date is a ballet dancer with a body that doesn't stop. She's going to get my ass kicked tonight, guaranteed. Heads turn and eyes follow as we weave through the dancing bodies. When we stop, she turns quickly and places my hands on her hips. I look around, checking to see what other guys are doing. They're sort of bobbing up and down, and of course the band has all the moves to get the ladies' attention.

Yvie doesn't want me to dance though as she rubs her ass hard against my groin. I groan, thankful that the loud music drowns out my weakness, and grip her hips a bit tighter. She moves, letting the music dictate what her body is doing. Her hands slide up and down my legs as she gyrates against me. She swivels her hips repeatedly until I have no choice but to follow her motions. It's an erotic display of affection with clothes on and I finally understand why guys do this. It gets you in the mood. Not that I need any help with that lately.

I'm afraid to let go for fear she'll move away from me. I loosen my grip, giving her a bit more freedom to maneuver against me. I tear my eyes from her briefly to see others watching, and I'm not sure if I should be enjoying this or not. By the looks on the other guys' faces, I should be. I'm starting to think each day with her is another fantasy come true, except this wasn't a fantasy... until now.

Her head falls back onto my shoulder and I press my mouth against the base of her neck, quickly working my way up to her ear. "You're making me hard."

She chuckles, knowing damn well that she's turning me on. Yvie continues what she's doing until the song is over. When she starts to walk away, I grab her and pull her to me. There is no way I can let her leave me just yet, not without a cover.

We stagger, meaning I walk awkwardly behind her thinking about everything from playing basketball to weight lifting. Except neither of those is doing me any good because I can picture Yvie in a cheerleading outfit, kicking her leg high up in the air and the weight bench... well I'll never look at another one of those the same again. Yvie somehow finds our friends and family over the mass of people. They look at us, some of them skeptical, and I avoid their gazes. I don't want to hear questions that I don't have answers for. Not tonight at least.

"You two look like you were having a good time out there," Harrison says before lifting his half-filled glass to his lips, never breaking eye contact. I can't tell if he's being serious or what.

"I knew you were tapping that arse," Jimmy laughs, earning a slap from Jenna. I shake my head and sit down, opposite Yvie.

"Where's Liam?" I direct my question toward Josie,

who is looking around. She finally shrugs.

"He's working, I guess."

I look at Harrison and Jimmy, who aren't saying anything.

"So, are you guys a couple?" Katelyn asks, her voice full of happiness.

I open my mouth to answer, but Yvie beats me to it. "We're just friends."

Ouch. Even though I've said it myself many times in my head, hearing her say it out loud hurts a lot worse than I imagined.

CHAPTER 15
YVIE

A S soon as the words are out of my mouth, I want to
take them back. I don't regret them because we're not
a couple, but I didn't mean them the way it sounds.
I'm somewhat thankful for the muted light drowning
out what I'm sure are awkward looks in my direction. I
can't look at Xander because I'm afraid of what I might
see. With the amount of time we've spent together I
know more of his expressions. He's either happy that I
confirmed that we're only friends, albeit with benefits at
the moment, or he's upset because he wants more. That's
the vibe I got from him when he picked me up at the
airport. I ignored the feeling though because I don't
want to make everything awkward between us. I want
to have fun and enjoy my self-imposed vacation. And
as selfish as it sounds, I want to have fun with Xander.
Adding unneeded pressure of what happens next will
only dampen our time together. There has to be a time

to discuss where each of us stands with what's going on. For all I know he doesn't want anything serious, and yes the obvious step is to ask, but I'm afraid of rejection. I also have to acknowledge that a part of me is hiding behind the fun we are having so that I don't have to make a decision as to what we are right now.

The waitress stops at our table and takes our orders. I look around the bar and marvel at all the people here to celebrate Liam and Josie's anniversary. I glance at Josie and have a bit of sympathy for her. Everyone is at the table except for Liam. Her eyes are focused on the beer bottle in front of her and she's not paying attention to anything going on around her. I turn back to the crowd and look for Liam. There are hundreds of people here, and while they're industry professionals, his wife should be by his side.

"I'll be right back," I say, before standing. I don't wait to see if anyone offers to come with me. This isn't a girls' trip to the bathroom, although maybe it should be. I meander through the crowd. There are some people I know and we stop and chat. For the most part, I grew up around some of these folks. When my mom worked for Liam's grandmother, she used to take us to parties at Betty's house. That was the only time we were allowed to attend though. Betty never cared that Harrison and I were there. She made us feel like family. I'm saddened to think about how much she's missed since she passed.

When I spot Liam, I ignore the people near me and make my way over to him. I pull him away from two men that I've never seen and right now don't care to meet.

"Yvie, what the fuck, I was talking to them?" He looks pissed, and I don't care. His wife, the one he vowed to spend the rest of his life with, is upset, and she should never sulk especially on their anniversary.

"What the fuck are you doing?" I accentuate my point my poking him in the chest.

Liam looks at me as if he's confused, but I know better. His dumb rocker persona doesn't fly with me. Never has, never will.

"It's my anniversary; why are you being mean to me?" His tone is brotherly. He's trying to smooth me over.

I drop my mouth in surprise. "What's the anniversary for?"

"Right, you weren't here, but I invited you. It's mine and Josie's anniversary. We were married on this day." He flashes his patent Liam Page smile, but I'm not buying it.

"It is?" I look at him with pure excitement and let him think I'm happy for him. Once he smiles, I scowl at him. "If it's your anniversary, where the hell is your wife?"

Liam's brows furrow as he looks down on me. "What are you talking about? She's sitting at our table."

I slap him across his chest and that earns a few gasps from the people near us. These people are probably calling *TMZ* right now and gossiping about Liam Page and Harrison James' sister arguing in the corner, although they'll likely turn it into a lover's quarrel.

"Your wife should be by your side, Liam. I know you're new to the whole relationship thing, but don't be dumb. She's over at the table looking sad and lost. Show her off for fuck's sake and stop being an ass." I look behind me quickly and notice that Xander has the same look as Josie. I need to fix my blunder from earlier. I can't leave him feeling like I don't care because I do. I don't know if Liam follows my eyes or not, but when I look back him, he's glaring at me.

"You sound like JD."

I throw my hands up in the air. "If that's all you got out of my little rant, then I feel sorry for you." I walk away, leaving him to figure out his own crap. I have my own to deal with and shouldn't even meddle in his life, but it pisses me off to see him working the room while Josie sits at the table being a fifth wheel to their friends. She should be by his side, standing there proudly with her husband.

Instead of going back to the table, I work my way through the crowd in search of the bathroom. Being my first time here, I'm not familiar with the layout, but most bars are the same – near the backdoor for an easy getaway. When I reach the restroom door, I bypass it for the door marked exit. I push it open and take a gulp of the cold air. I need a breather.

The cold air chills my body temperature and helps me relax. I lean up against the wall and put my head back. Closing my eyes, I imagine that it's snowing. If I were home in New York, I'd be ice skating or walking down Fifth Avenue with my friends. We'd call it an early night though because of the show. We'd make plans to meet in the morning before rehearsals. There's nothing like the holiday season in New York City, and I'm sorry that I missed it, but on the other hand I'm thankful because I spent the time with my family, and I needed that.

As soon as the door opens, I know it's someone coming to get me. My first thought is Xander and my immediate thought after that is what it'd be like to have him take me against this wall. That shouldn't be the first thought that crosses my mind. I should want to see him for him, not because of the way he makes me feel during sex.

When heels appear, I breathe a sigh of relief. It's Katelyn, who happens to be carrying my clutch, followed by Jenna.

"Thanks," I say, as I reach for my clutch. Katelyn stands next to me and Jenna lingers. The only thing missing from this scene are cigarettes and martinis. I sigh, and close my eyes. I don't want to ask them what they're doing out here, or why they aren't with Josie or even the guys.

"What's going on with you?" Katelyn asks.

My eyes fling open. "What do you mean?"

Katelyn turns to face me. "I know I don't know you very well, and honestly I'm out here because Harrison said you needed girl time. Jenna and I like our girl time so I told him we'd come check on you."

"How'd you know where I was?"

"Xander knew," Jenna adds with a shrug. How did he know? Was he following me?

"Harrison thinks you're acting strange, and that it has something to do with my question earlier. I didn't mean to put you on the spot or anything. You and Xander just looked really comfortable together."

"It's fine," I tell her. I'm not angry or embarrassed. Xander is a catch and wouldn't be single if he lived in New York or even California. Guys like him, genuine and caring, are hard to come by in the big city.

"He likes you." I look at Jenna who shrugs. "He told Jimmy, or that's what Jimmy said."

I roll my eyes. "Jimmy is full of shit, always has been. Xander and I are just having fun."

"Is that all you're having?" Katelyn asks. Her voice is hushed as if someone could hear her. I look around to see who is lurking, but spot no one.

"Jimmy said you recently broke up with your boyfriend," Jenna adds.

"His name is Oliver, and he's my producer as well. We've been off and on for a while, and I just made it off." I take a deep breath and center myself. "Things with Oliver were good in the beginning. I thought I was in love, but the more time we spent together the more I realized he wasn't the right man for me. Breaking up though, it's not that easy when you work with someone. We'd get into a fight, and I'd suddenly be too fat and my hair wasn't done right.

"Oliver likes to manipulate me and used my spot as the lead to get me to do what he wants and that's being with him. When I broke up with him this last time, I boarded a plane. He hasn't called or texted so I figured he got the gist."

"Is that why you're here and not back in New York, which I might add completely threw your brother for a loop when he saw you guys walk in tonight?" Katelyn asks.

My shoulders shrug. "I got a text from a friend about Oliver and I thought 'why waste my time' and happened to catch Xander before he got too far from the airport. He asked me to be his date tonight." I trail off, my voice seems sad and I'm not sure why that is.

"So, what's the problem?" Jenna asks. Maybe it's obvious to her that something is wrong. I just don't know what.

"I'm not sure," I say, honestly. "If I could clone myself, I would. I'd go back to New York and stay here and see where things go."

"With Xander?" Katelyn asks.

I nod. "Xander is different. Even in the week we've been hanging out, he treats me better than Oliver. But he's here," I say, with a shrug.

The door opens and we all turn our heads. I glance at Katelyn and Jenna, who are both trying to see back inside.

"You guys go on; I'll be there in a minute."

"You sure?" Katelyn asks with a sisterly concern.

"Yeah, I'm good."

As soon as the door shuts, the muffled sound of my cell phone can be heard. Unzipping my clutch, I can't help but smile at the thought of Xander calling me. He must've seen the girls walk back in and wonder about me. I wouldn't mind if he came out here, we could have some fun. I fumble getting my phone out and end up answering before I can see his face on my screen.

"I've been waiting for you. There's a nice wall out here that has our name on it."

"Does it now? And where would such a wall be since you're clearly not in your apartment?"

I close my eyes at the sound of Oliver's voice and mentally curse my stupid clutch for being just a smidge too small to hold my phone. My heart beats loudly, echoing in my ear.

"Yvie, answer me."

I don't want to, but he knows I will. "I'm in Beaumont."

"You were due home the day after Christmas. Clearly, you've met someone."

I bite the inside of my cheek and nod knowing he can't see me. "It's none of your business. We broke up, and you moved on."

"On the contrary, my lovely, little ballerina. You tried to break up with me, but I won't allow it and I don't know what Lindsay told you, but she's mistaken."

"She saw you with Cami, said that Cami has been practicing in my spot."

Oliver laughs, and it chills my bones. "Cami is your understudy. She needs the practice."

"In more ways than one, I'm sure."

"Such a flippant attitude you have."

I roll my eyes and count to ten. "I'm at a party; I need to go. I'll call you when I get home."

"Which will be when? I miss you and need to be with you."

I shake my head and don't answer, ending the call and turning off my phone. I have to be stronger than the person I am when he's around. I need to be the confident woman I am when I'm with Xander. *That* woman wouldn't take Oliver's shit.

CHAPTER 16
XANDER

LOOK around the gym and count maybe five people in here. A few are the meatheads, the power lifters, hoisting some weights before they go drink themselves into a stupor. Their New Year's Resolutions will actually start on the second, after they've had a day to detox. Tonight, they want the tighter muscles to show through their skintight shirts. It's a trick all the guys use. Pound out a few reps before you go on a date. When you think you might score, hit the bathroom and get a few push-ups in before you take off your shirt. Girls have been known to do it as well, but with guys it's obvious.

It's been snowing on and off today, creating just enough slush outside that boots are required. Growing up in Florida, I didn't have many opportunities to see snow until I went off to college. I attended the University of Delaware for physical therapy, and the first time it snowed there I didn't know what to do. My buddies all laughed at me and took me shopping after class. I had to outfit an entire wardrobe just to get through the cold winters. Shorts and flip-flops weren't going to cut it. The weather can ruin a lot of plans, and I'm wondering how tonight is going to shape up.

I'm taking Yvie out, or better yet, she's taking me. She asked me to be her date for tonight and I happily accepted. She's going home tomorrow. She's assured me that I'll be rid of her just after the New Year. Thing is, I'm not ready for her to leave. I like having her around, and I especially like that she has come into the gym the past few days. After Liam and Josie's anniversary party, I took her back to Harrison's where she still had a car. She wanted to stay there, and I understood. She wants to get to know the twins and this extra time is important to her. Still, I wouldn't mind waking up next to her, but right now I'll take whatever I can get.

Yvie left about an hour ago. She walked out of here promising me a night to remember. Little does she know that just being in the same room with her, or holding her hand is all I really need. Being the gym owner has its perks, but not when you're the only one working. Since the first night here, I've had thoughts of taking her on my desk, having my arm sweep everything off as her hands pull at my clothes. She's adventurous, I'll give her that. And flexible. I have a whole new appreciation for a ballet barre now that I've been able to use it for something fun. I want to make a New Year's resolution, but having it fail doesn't appeal. If either of us lived in the same city, it'd be easy to sit down and tell her that I want more. That we owe it to ourselves to give us a chance. Right now, my resolution would be to make sure she's always smiling and for her to know that I'm a phone call away.

The gym is going to feel empty without her, but

I'm trying not to think about it. Having Yvie here and working out brought a spark to me. Other members have noticed it, but I played it off telling them it was because of the holidays; no one needs to know the truth – I've fallen for the girl. I'll make sure everything goes back to normal. She's not my girlfriend. I have to remind myself of this fact daily, but Yvie makes me smile, and we have an amazing time together. This past week has been refreshing and one of my best weeks ever. I owe that all to her and when she leaves tomorrow, I'll do the same as I did on Christmas night. I'll walk into the airport with her and say goodbye.

We've made no promises to each other, other than texting and calling occasionally. I don't know where her head's at with her ex. It's not like he's a normal ex, one that goes away when you break-up; he's her boss. She's going to see him and as much as I want to pound his face with my fist and ask her to stay away from him, I'm can't. Believe me, thoughts of flying to New York to confront the loser have played through my mind many times. I've even looked at flights. But Yvie is too important to me to do that. I can't jeopardize her career because of my overbearing ego and the need to protect what's mine… or what I want to be mine.

The door chimes and JD walks in. I nod to him and turn my attention to the paperwork sitting on the counter. I'm supposed to be going over the new memberships and making sure they're all in order before they're entered into the computer. The last thing I need here is for an error to mess up everything.

"What's up, mate?"

I look up; JD looks concerned. His brows are furrowed, and he seems distracted.

"What's going on?" I put the paperwork to one side

and give him my full attention.

JD looks around, peering over both his shoulders before he leans over the counter. "I was playing with Little One outside, and my chest tightened. I didn't think anything of it, but then it hurt to breathe."

I lean back and try to read more from his expression. The harder I look, the more I see fear. His doctor said that he would experience times where breathing would be difficult, but he hadn't had any issues yet. I thought he was in the clear.

"Have you called your doctor?" I ask, hoping that he has a cold or the beginning of one.

JD shakes his head. "What if he says something's wrong?"

Sitting forward, I fold my hands together. His fears are legitimate. He had a life-threatening injury and by all accounts probably shouldn't have survived. JD went through extensive physical therapy to rebuild his lungs and worked hard to be free of any walking devices before Eden was born. If he's having a setback, this could kill him, so to speak.

"I think you need to call the doctor and see if you can get in. Tell him that you want an x-ray and make sure you share your concerns with him."

JD contemplates what I'm saying and nods. "What if I need more therapy?"

I shrug nonchalantly. "If you do, we'll do it. I can easily make adjustments in my schedule to accommodate you. But it may just be a cold, or the cold air."

"You're coming with us on tour, right? I know you said you would, but I just need to make sure."

I nod. "You won't need me, but I'll be there."

"All right, mate. I should probably get home. I told Jenna I was going out to buy some milk. I don't even know if we need milk."

"Don't worry, JD. You look fine, other than the stress of freaking yourself out. I'll see ya tonight, man." JD and I man-shake by ways of a fist-bump and he takes his leave.

I can't even imagine what kind of fear he lives with each time he thinks something could be wrong. I'm not sure what I can do to curb that fear, but I'm going to try.

M Y front door opens and closes quickly. I set down my half-full soda can on the counter and walk slowly into my living room. When I round the corner, I'm welcomed by the most beautiful sight, yet the most confusing.

Yvie is bent over, untying her tennis shoes. Sweatpants cover her legs and her small frame is hidden behind my way-too-big-for-her sweatshirt. By all accounts she should be dressed, and ready to head to *Ralph's* to ring in the New Year. If this is her attire, I'm way overdressed.

I clear my throat and her head pops up. Her smile spreads from ear to ear and its nothing but mischievous. I can't help but smile while I wait for her to finish taking off her shoes.

"Is there a magic dress under those sweats?"

Yvie stands, walks over to me and places her hands on my chest. "Nope," she says. "Under these sweats you'll find nothing but me."

Placing my hands on her hips, I lean down and place a kiss on the tip of her nose. "Is tonight some type of costume party?"

She shakes her head and takes my face in her hands, placing a long, lingering kiss on my lips. I follow her as she pulls away, not ready to end our kiss. When I open my eyes, she's smiling, and it hits me that this is our last night together.

"I thought we'd stay in. I got to thinking when I was packing that the last thing I want to do is go out to a bar where it's noisy and crowded, when all I really want to do is cuddle up next to you on the couch and watch movies."

"Yeah?" I ask, making sure that my ears aren't deceiving me.

"Yeah. I mean unless you want to go out. I can change–"

"No, no, this is great. Fantastic even. I'd love to sit on the couch and watch movies with you."

Yvie's face lights up, and I try to memorize the look of excitement on her face. There are so many moments that I wish I had a camera so that when she's gone, I can go back and look at them and bring up each memory. Some of her expressions I won't be able to replicate over Skype.

"I brought essentials," she says, walking away from me. She bends over, and I find my head tilting to the side to get a good look at her beautiful ass. Yvie's been working hard to firm up and I've been helping.

Yvie turns her head quickly and catches me staring at her. Her grin is wicked as she winks at me. When she stands, she's holding a bottle of wine.

"The only thing missing is food," I say, as she walks past me and into the kitchen.

"I thought we could get take out."

I pretend to ponder the idea, but pull out the take-out menus and hand them to her. I trap her against the counter and nuzzle her neck. She giggles, but doesn't pull away.

"How about Chinese?"

"Perfect," I murmur against her neck.

After calling in our order, I open the bottle of wine and pour us a glass each.

"To a new year and new friends," I say, as our glasses touch.

"And midnight kisses," she says, pulling my glass away and bringing me in for a kiss.

CHAPTER 17
YVIE

WARMTH. *That's what I feel when I'm nestled in Xander's arms. He's allowed me to channel surf. He hasn't balked once, even when I stop on the sappy movies. He encourages me to change the channel and kisses away my blubbering tears when I don't.*

"I don't understand why you watch this if it's going to make you cry." *He adjusts me in his arms, resting his head on top of my shoulder. His arms are wrapped around me as I sit between his legs. A blanket, one that his mom made, covers his legs.*

"Tell me about your parents." *I know this is a line we shouldn't cross, but he knows so much about my family, and I know nothing about his. We're not in a relationship, but we're friends and friends can know things. At least that's what I'm telling myself.*

"What do you want to know?" *Xander brushes his fingers along the nape of my neck causing not only goosebumps, but also a change in body temperature. I know what he wants. I want it too. It's our last night together and both of us have avoided the elephant in the room – when or if we'll see each other again. I want to see him. I'm just not sure how to make it work. I don't know if Xander fits in with the life I lead in New York. I had a hard enough time fitting in here. I'm just not sure how long I'll be able to stay away. Aside from my family, I really enjoy being with Xander. I just don't know if I can give him what I think he needs in life.*

"What do they do, names, where do they live?"

"Ah, are we at that stage now?" Before I can answer, his fingers tighten over my shoulders and he starts to knead my muscles. My head falls back, and I let out the longest moan ever.

"Hmm, I sort of like that sound," he whispers against my skin.

"Xander, tell me."

He sighs, but doesn't stop with the massage. His fingers and hands are like magic and could put me to sleep, although I know that won't happen. Not tonight.

"My dad is a financial advisor and my mom is an interior decorator. They live in Miami is an obscenely large home that most of us refer to as a mansion. They work long hours, cater to the stars and vacation a lot."

I'm a little taken by how well off his parents seem to be. By all accounts, Xander should be a stuck up party boy living off his parent's money, but he's not. He's grounded, with a good head on his shoulders and with a thriving business.

"Do they know the guys?" By guys, I mean Liam, my brother and Jimmy.

"Hmm, I'm not sure. They could, or maybe Liam knows someone who knows them. We've never discussed it, and I'd *never use my parents to get ahead in life."*

I nod, and lean back into him a little more. He stops rubbing my shoulders, and instead wraps me in his arms.

"Do you like your job? What about your parents, do they like that you live in Beaumont?"

"When I answered the ad for JD, I never thought it would lead to all of this. I was just a few years out of college and working in a rehab facility when I happened to see the ad that the administrator posted from the job website. It said that it could be twenty-four hours, and that the applicant must be willing to travel, all expenses taken care of. I thought, what the hell? I'm young and have nothing holding me back so I answered. The phone interview wasn't even with Liam, and I really had no idea who I was going to work for until he called me one day.

"I'd love to buy one of the old buildings downtown and renovate it with businesses on the bottom and some nice apartments above them. I'm thinking more high-end to maybe bring in bigger business and help the economy thrive. Either way, my parents are on board. My dad is the silent owner of the gym. Everything is in my name, but he's there in the event of a financial crisis, not that I see that happening anytime soon."

Xander places his lips against my neck, telling me that he's done talking about his life. His arms tighten, holding me to him.

"Do you like this movie?" he asks, knowing full well that even if I do I'm going to give him my full attention.

"I've seen it before. What do you have in mind?"

His fingers find the edge of my cami, his sweatshirt that I wore here, long forgotten. My cami is lifted over my head and tossed to the ground.

"I'm thinking you and the bottle of champagne on the table."

I turn and look at him. "Me, the table and the bottle?"

He nods as a serious look comes over his face. "I plan to lick the champagne off your body."

I look at him questioningly, my eyebrow rise. He matches my expression. "Do you have an issue with that?"

He gently pushes us to the edge of the couch and stands us up. Xander takes my hand in his and leads us into the kitchen. Earlier, after dinner, he cleaned off the table. I didn't think anything of it, but now I know it's because he had this planned.

"How long have you thought about doing this?"

He shrugs. "I bought the champagne earlier because I thought we'd celebrate after getting back from the bar, but holding you in my arms and knowing that I have this fantasy to play out, I thought we should try it."

I let go of his hand and cross my arms. "And what about me? Do I get to do shots off your abs?"

Xander smirks and lifts up his shirt, showing me his perfectly sculpted stomach. "I got the tequila right here, baby," he points to the cabinet behind him.

I stand tall. "Bring it on."

"Excuse me miss." I startle awake, only to find the flight attendant hovering over me. "We're about to land. I need you to put your chair in its upright position."

I do as she says and rub the sleep away from my eyes. I don't remember taking off, and I'm not sure if that's a good or bad thing. The dream, reliving last night and this morning, is something I definitely didn't want to wake-up from. Being with Xander, experimenting with him the way we have, has shown me what sex can really mean when it's between two people who care about each other. I know I can go to him with anything and hope he feels the same way about me.

What Xander and I have is special and can't be replicated.

As soon as I step out of the taxi, my boot is submerged ankle deep in a puddle. I glance at the driver who is ignoring me by playing on his phone. It's not like I expected him to get out and help me, but a little curiosity would be nice. After heaving myself out of the cab, I reach in and pull out my luggage and stuff a twenty through his plastic window security divider. My door isn't even shut before he's pulling away and into traffic with the sounds of horns honking. I wish the police would start pulling people over for violating the no honking ordinance. The day they do, I'm going to get a chair and start flashing people simply for the entertainment.

I look down at my soaked boot and shake my foot. "Welcome home," I say to no one as I sigh and turn toward my building. I stare at the gloomy building, wishing the corporation that owns it would paint the outside, give it new life. But no, we're stuck with this gray monstrosity that I call home. Climbing the three steps with my carry on dragging behind me, I stop at the doorman's desk, the same doorman who is supposed to open our entrance door, but is too old to move about. He's also supposed to be security, but the only thing he's good for is a great laugh, hug and making sure our mail is ready for us when we walk in.

"Hello, Charles, how was your Christmas?"

"Oh, Miss Yvie, my Christmas was very good. It's good to see you back home."

I pause at the word home. You never realize how often you throw that word around and what it really means. When I was growing up, our tiny apartment was home until we moved into a slightly larger one, and so on. Even Harrison's apartment on the beach felt like home. This is where I live and, up until this past week, I always thought of it as home, except now I know it's not. Home means family, and I don't have that here. I'm not saying I'm packing up and moving to Beaumont, but visiting more often or having my nephew and nieces here might help.

I'm not ready to leave New York. Right now, it feels like it's all I know. It's where my job is, and I love my job. I know I can dance elsewhere, but it's not same as Broadway. I need the best of both worlds. I need my Beaumont family and my New York job to meld into one.

"Thanks, it's good to be back, and thanks for my mail."

I hadn't realized that my mental musing was a time lapse. In the time it took me to respond to Charles, he had already retrieved my mail. I need to shift my focus back to work and how I'm going to deal with Oliver. I'm not naïve enough to think that tomorrow is going to be a cake walk. I know I'm going to have to fight for my spot, which I find ludicrous. We don't re-open for another week, and it's not like our routine has changed.

"Have a good night, Miss Yvie."

I wave and make my way to the elevator. Once inside, I press the button to the eighth floor and wait. It's slow moving, but better than walking up the flights of stairs. I could move, but I like my place. It's a one-bedroom with a small kitchen and living room. The view is fantastic and I have access to the fire escape where I sit during the summer and people watch. I think that's one of my favorite things to do – people watch.

Tonight, lights brighten the dark streets and passersby mingle in front of the stores and buildings that still have their displays up. They'll start coming down tomorrow and just like that, the holiday season is over. Everyone will forget for months about how stressful and wonderful the past few weeks have been, until it starts all over again. I won't forget. I have too many memories, and each time I close my eyes, Xander is right there reminding me of everything we shared.

The knock on my door doesn't surprise me. I know it's Oliver before I even open it. He often frequents the coffee shop across the street, especially when we're not getting along. I don't know why he feels that this is like the other times before. Breaking up with him and leaving was the best decision to make. Being away gave me time to see what my life is like without him. I didn't sit around and pine for him, or even call him. I used the time to connect with my family. I experienced what it was like to be free and let myself go, and when I did I was rewarded with Xander, a man who sees me for me and isn't pressuring me to be someone I don't want to be.

Oliver knocks again causing me to roll my eyes. Charles, no doubt, confirmed that I am indeed, home. Charles doesn't know any better, but Oliver does. He knows that I don't have anything to say.

As I look at the door, I see that I didn't lock it. That's not something I usually forget. I know my mind is elsewhere, maybe still in Beaumont. I open the door, standing between it and the doorjamb. Oliver is resting against the opposite wall. The look on his face is pensive. He's thinking and showing me that he's hurt. If he would look at me he'd see that I don't care. Not anymore.

"I'm happy to see you've finally decided to come home."

I sigh and fight the urge to roll my eyes. "We aren't scheduled to rehearse until tomorrow. I'm home."

"Most performers rehearse day in and day out to make sure that when the curtain goes up they're ready. They don't take a two week vacation and come back like nothing has changed."

"Everything has changed, Oliver. What did you think? That I would stay home and sulk, waiting for you to call? Not this time. I told you, I'm done." I move to shut the door, but he stops me. I could fight him. I could yell and scream and the guy down the hall will come running or the lady across from me will call 911 without even opening her door, but he's harmless. When I say Oliver is the quintessential Broadway producer, he is. He's a pretty metro boy who cares more about his appearance than lifting weights. His weekly mani-pedi's are a must for him.

"Yvie, you don't mean this. Sure, we've hit a rough patch, but once you come to your senses, everything will be better."

I throw my hands up. "To my senses? What does that mean?"

"Marriage, Yvie. We could become a powerhouse couple, and you keep pushing it off."

I rub my temples and wish I hadn't answered the door. I'm going on a lack of sleep. I'm exhausted and really just want to crawl into bed.

"I need some sleep, Oliver. I'll see you tomorrow at rehearsals." I walk toward the open door and hold it, motioning for him to leave.

"And we'll talk tomorrow?"

I let him think that I'm contemplating his offer. He steps out of my apartment thinking that he's won again. I look at him as I start to close the door. "Oliver, it's over," I say as I slam the door quickly and slide the lock in place. Resting my head against the door, I wait until I hear his footsteps move down the hall. I pull out my cell phone and bring it to life. My background picture is of Xander and me at three a.m. this morning, lying on his bed. My head is on his shoulder and my hand on his chest. We were looking at each other as he took the picture. I don't know what possessed me to set it as my background, but

I'm happy that I did.

I pull up his name, my thumb hovering over the letters as if they're able to be touched. As if he knows I'm thinking about him, a text pops up from him.

Xander: Did you make it home?

Just knowing he cares makes me smile and makes my heart hurt. It'd be so easy to give in to him and not look back.

I'm home, door is locked and my bed is screaming my name.

Xander: You were screaming my name pretty loud a few hours ago.

I don't know how he does it, but a simple look from him and I'm a wanton whore, lifting my skirt in the car just so I can have one more time with him before I had to leave.

I know. I haven't forgotten.

Xander: I meant to ask you earlier – when can I see you next?

My heart beats a little faster knowing that he wants to see me and is already asking. I just don't know what the answer is. I think that if I leave the ball in his court, I'm not faced with saying something stupid or out of place.

I work five nights a week, but I can take time off. It's usually no more than 2 days.

I press send before I can change my reply. He needs to know that my job is important to me even though I want to see him.

> **Xander: You know, I've been thinking... well, I'm just thinking! Good night, Tiny Dancer.**

I stare at my phone, wondering if I should reply. Part of me wants to know what he's thinking and the other part wants to be surprised, romanced. Xander is definitely someone who can romance me.

CHAPTER 18
XANDER

IT'S been six-weeks since I dropped Yvie off at the airport for a second time and not a day has gone by where I haven't thought about her. I can't look at the weight bench without memories of *that* night flooding my mind and have thought about moving it into my office and replacing it with another. Even though I sterilized it, I cringe each time someone uses it, out of jealousy and for sanitary reasons.

It's hard telling myself that Yvie and I are just friends and that we're not a couple. From the outside, I'm sure that's all we look like, but according to my phone bill over ninety percent of my calls, both incoming and outgoing, are with her. We've logged who knows how many hours on video chat and she's my first and last text message of each and every day. It'd be stupid of me to try and push her to define what we are, though. My hope is that when she's ready, she'll tell me. My fear, however, is that when she says she's ready, it will be with someone else. I have to find a way to get out of this friend zone and more into the "this is the guy I'm seeing" zone, even if we do live thousands of miles away.

Over the past few weeks, I've learned so much about Yvie James. I know her best friend, Lindsay, hates Oliver (secretly I do, too) and is encouraging Yvie to find a different production to perform in. She doesn't ask for my opinion, and I'm okay with that. I can't act like I'm jealous because she has to spend every day with her ex-boyfriend/producer douche, even though I am. It's her job, just as my job as a personal trainer puts me in contact with a lot of very nice looking females. Those females don't hold a candle to Yvie, though, and as many times as I've told her that, I can still hear the jealousy in her voice. It's a hazard of both our jobs, and probably a hang up for the both of us. It's definitely something we'd need to overcome if we were to make this official.

I want to make us official, but not while we're living apart. I can't ask her to move, and uprooting my life here doesn't seem feasible. I've established a reputable business, not to mention my commitment to JD's recovery. His recent scare with his chest pains has me concerned. Not that I'd share those concerns with him. Leaving here doesn't make sense in my eyes, and Yvie moving here likely doesn't make sense in hers. I'm afraid that she and I are both in limbo, hanging on by a thread in the friend zone.

As I look out, people are bundled up to ward off the mid-winter chill. Ice skaters move by café windows, showing off their talents for all those who sit inside and watch. My skates are on and laced up and my pea coat buttoned up. Jenna said I needed this coat and that my sweatshirt wouldn't cut it if I'm going to try to fit in. I don't want to fit in, but I don't want to be an embarrassment either.

The horn sounds telling the ice skaters to leave the ice and my nerves start to take over. I've never done anything like this, something spontaneous and so forthcoming. I'm either going to walk away a happy man for a few days, or with my tail between my legs. Ask me last week and I could have assured you that I was doing the right thing. Ask me right now and I'll tell you that my legs are shaking, and my knees are knocking together.

The next session of skaters move out onto the ice under the night sky. As I step out of the café, I can't help but feel the magic. The holidays are over, but the rink and outer areas are still fully alive with life and color.

I spot Yvie easily, thanks to Lindsay's stealth planning. The day I got an email from Lindsay about Yvie, I knew I had to do something drastic, yet endearing, so she knows that I want to be in this for the long haul if she's willing. Lindsay found me through my website and filled me in on how much Yvie is missing me. For the first time, I felt my hope soar that Yvie and I could have a future. I never went as far to ask for details because I didn't want Lindsay to betray Yvie's confidence, but the message was received loud and clear. Lindsay and I worked together to get me to New York.

Pulling out my phone, I text Yvie. **What're you doing tonight?**

I see the exact moment she takes out her phone. Her skates slow down and she removes one of her gloves to text me back. If the ice rink were more crowded, I'd be in trouble.

Tiny Dancer: Nothing :(just hanging with Lindsay. You?

Her text stabs me deep because there are so many times I wanted to tell her my plans, but the girls told me to keep it a secret. They all said the surprise would be worth it.

As soon as Yvie and Lindsay skate by, I step out onto the ice and head to the center. I've had this grand scheme mapped out for weeks, but I'll be damned if I remember what I'm supposed to be doing. Lindsay has a part and for the love of all things holy I hope she remembers. When I see Yvie again, her face is down and she's moving along with the crowd. The smile she had earlier is gone and I can't help but hope it's because we're not together.

I look around and see that I'm not the only guy standing in the center. Apparently my idea isn't as original as I thought, but I can't change it now. Lindsay sees me in position and directs Yvie to the spot where I'm standing and bumps her shoulder. When Yvie looks up, her mouth drops open as her hand quickly covers it. Her beautiful eyes are now filling with unshed tears and she starts to shake her head. I stand there, speechless, extending to her a single red rose. There are more roses, red and white ones, covering her apartment thanks to Charles, her doorman, and Lindsay.

"Yvie, will you be my Valentine?" I ask her, my voice breaking. There's a moment of silence when she doesn't say anything, and it feels like time has stopped while I wait for her reaction.

"Say yes!" someone yells and she sort of laughs and coughs at the same time.

Yvie pulls her hand away and reaches for me. "What are you doing here?" her voice breaks and teeters between excitement and dare I say tears, albeit happy ones.

I shake my head. "Well, it's a holiday and we've spent all our holidays together. I couldn't let one get skipped, now could I?"

Yvie slides her arms around my waist and buries her head into my scarf. I hate that I'm wearing it because I want to feel her against my skin. I hold her to me, basking in these few minutes that I can have her in my arms again.

"I can't believe you're here," Yvie tells me as she lifts her head. She places her hands, one freezing cold and the other gloved, on my cheeks and holds my gaze. "I know I shouldn't say it, but I've missed you." Before I can respond, her lips press against mine. She moves against me with such urgency, with such need that I choose to let her guide us. When she deepens the kiss, I pull her as tight as I can, eager to feel her against my body. The catcalls cause me to pull away. She lives and works here, and doesn't need to be recognized as that woman who made out on the ice rink.

"What'd you say we take this someplace else?" I ask, hoping that she says her place since that's where all my stuff is.

"My apartment isn't far; we could walk. It's a nice night out."

I look up and see how bright everything is in the night sky. The lights of Manhattan could guide you anywhere. Thoughts of holding her hand while we walk the streets flash through my mind. It's something I want to do. "That sounds great."

YVIE doesn't let go of my hand or my arm throughout our walk to her apartment. Every few feet, she stops and pulls me in for a kiss or we stop and she talks about a church or tells me what building we're passing. As much as I want to explore Manhattan, there's time for that later. Besides, she's far more interesting. Tonight, I want to hold her, sit on her couch with my arm wrapped around her shoulder while she nestles into me. Tomorrow, I'll happily follow her around as she gives me a tour of the city she loves.

She stands on the first step leading to her apartment building and rests her hands on the back of my neck. The look in her eyes is one of excitement and, I hope, longing. I can only hope my features match hers.

"I can't believe you're here. Are you real?"

"I'm real. I can show you later if you'd like." My eyebrows dance, earning an eye roll from her but also a wicked little smile.

"Come on, let's go inside. I have a nice warm apartment that I want you to see." I was pleasantly surprised at how much like Yvie her apartment is. The moment I stepped in, I knew she lived there. I don't know what I expected, but when I walked in it felt like I was wrapped in her arms. Her place is quaint and perfect for a single person. The colors on her walls are warm and inviting. Her shelves and walls are adorned with photos of her dancing and of her family. There are a lot of pictures of her with the band, with her and Harrison, but mostly of her and Quinn.

Once inside the building, she walks us up to the front desk.

"Miss Yvie, I hope you had a nice evening." Charles, the man behind the desk, smiles brightly at her. You can tell that he cares about her deeply.

"Oh, Charles, it's been the best night. I want you to meet Xander," she says with her hand on my chest. My heart beats rapidly as I gaze down at her. She has to know she does this to me.

Charles and I shake hands, acting as if we haven't met already. "It's nice to meet you, Charles."

"You too, Mr. Xander." Charles is a professional and doesn't let on. It will only take a few seconds for Yvie to realize that those close to her knew about this and helped me pull it off.

I hold Yvie in the elevator. She holds my hand when we exit, and I have to fight every urge not to lead the way. Each second it takes her to slide in her keys and open the door is painstakingly slow.

My throat tightens when she steps in. This is a risk and something I've never done before, but Jenna said Yvie would love it. Jenna hooked me up with a florist nearby who had the roses ready for me when I arrived. Once Lindsay and Yvie left, Lindsay sent me a quick text and Charles let me in. He even helped spread the rose petals, saying Yvie deserves nothing but the best. I happen to agree and hope that she thinks that's me.

Yvie turns on the light and gasps. I step in and stand next to her, afraid to say anything.

"You did this?"

I nod, and look around the room. The red and white rose petals are scattered around her living room. On her little end table sits a bottle of champagne in a bucket of ice. The strawberries are in her refrigerator.

"I had a little help," I say, shrugging.

Yvie shakes her head. "How did you do all of this?"

I start to take off my coat and she follows. She takes mine and hangs it in the closet with hers. The benefit of a small apartment is that she's not that far out of reach and her hand is back in mine before I know it.

"Sit down," I say, kissing her nose. "Let me grab a few things."

I walk into the kitchen and pull out the strawberries and pick up the two champagne flutes I bought earlier.

Yvie is looking at the vases of roses, four in total,

which are around her living room. I pop the cork and the bubbly spills over, causing her to laugh.

"I've always wanted to see that."

"It must be your lucky night," I say as I hand her a glass of champagne.

"Are you going to fill me in?"

"Yes, let's sit though." I bring over the strawberries and sit next to her. As soon as she takes a sip, I offer her a strawberry.

"Mhm, this taste so good." She moans, and I ache a little more inside. This is why long distance relationships are hard when you're so attracted to someone. Something as simple as eating a piece of fruit is a turn on.

"Yes, I had help," I say, before running the strawberry over her lips. "Lindsay emailed me. She said she thought you were lonely and suggested I visit. I miss you, so here I am. Lindsay was kind enough to get me in touch with Charles, and Jenna helped me with the flowers."

Yvie's eyes water and she buries her face into my chest. I use the opportunity to hold her. "I'm sorry, I didn't mean to upset you."

She shakes her head. "You didn't," she mumbles. "You make every romantic theory come true, and I think you do it without even trying."

"Um… is that good?" I hate that I even have to ask, but I'm a dude. I don't know much about romance.

She lifts up her head and smiles. "It's very good." She stands and pulls my hand into hers. "Come on, I want to show you my room." She winks.

"But we have champagne," I say, as I stand.

"Do you still have abs?"

I laugh and pull my shirt from my pants so she can see.

"Well, I say bring it so I can put those abs to use. I've

missed them."

'Yeah, they've missed you too' I want to say, but plan to save that line for later. I follow her into her room with the bottle of champagne and bowl of strawberries. The only thing missing is whipped cream, but I can pick that up tomorrow.

"Happy Valentine's Day."

ABOUT THE AUTHOR

Heidi is a *New York Times* and *US Today* bestselling author.

Originally from the Pacific Northwest, she now lives in picturesque Vermont, with her husband and two daughters. Also renting space in their home is an overhyper Beagle/Jack Russell and two Parakeets.

During the day you'll find her behind a desk talking about Land Use. At night, she's writing one of the many stories she plans to release or sitting courtside during either daughter's basketball games.

She's also an active book reviewer on The Readiacs.

Connect with Heidi:

Twitter: www.twitter.com/HeidiJoVT
Facebook: www.facebook.com/
HeidiMcLaughlinAuthor
Blog: heidimclaughlinauthor.blogspot.com

9 781507 569092